"Tasting _____"
he said

"You need to take your time and give it all your attention."

Jess lifted the glass, but Michael reached for her hand and stopped her before the glass reached her lips.

"Let it slide over your tongue and around the inside of your mouth before you swallow it." Her insides went wobbly. His voice had taken on a sinfully deep tone and she swore it was reverberating through his hand and up her arm. "Try it."

She took a sip and so did he. She watched his mouth, and didn't swallow until he did.

"What do you think?"

Jess was at a loss for words, and that almost never happened. Instead of answering, she just smiled, took another slow, careful sip of wine and imagined she was being kissed.

Dear Reader,

I've always enjoyed learning new things and visiting new places, so doing research for a book is one of the things that makes writing so much fun. That's been especially true with this, my second book set in San Francisco. I love the city's dynamic neighborhoods, but this story also took me outside the city and into Northern California's beautiful wine country. And of course that required research.

Setting provides that all-important backdrop for any book, but as the story in *The Wedding Bargain* emerged, the contrast between the clamor and commotion of the city and the order and symmetry of Napa Valley's vineyards was reflected in the power of family ties, two people's determination to succeed and the struggle that ensues when they want the same thing but believe only one of them can have it.

In spite of their different backgrounds, Jess and Michael do have some common ground—they both believe family matters more than anything else. I had a lot of fun writing their story, so I hope you enjoy reading it. As always, readers can visit me through my website at www.leemckenzie.com, where you'll find links to my Facebook page and my blog, The Writer Side of Life.

Happy reading!

Lee McKenzie

The Wedding Bargain
LEE McKENZIE

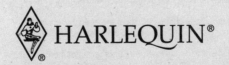

HARLEQUIN®

TORONTO • NEW YORK • LONDON
AMSTERDAM • PARIS • SYDNEY • HAMBURG
STOCKHOLM • ATHENS • TOKYO • MILAN • MADRID
PRAGUE • WARSAW • BUDAPEST • AUCKLAND

Recycling programs
for this product may
not exist in your area.

ISBN-13: 978-0-373-75344-4

THE WEDDING BARGAIN

Copyright © 2011 by Lee McKenzie McAnally

All rights reserved. Except for use in any review, the reproduction or
utilization of this work in whole or in part in any form by any electronic,
mechanical or other means, now known or hereafter invented, including
xerography, photocopying and recording, or in any information storage
or retrieval system, is forbidden without the written permission of the
publisher, Harlequin Enterprises Limited, 225 Duncan Mill Road,
Don Mills, Ontario M3B 3K9, Canada.

This is a work of fiction. Names, characters, places and incidents are
either the product of the author's imagination or are used fictitiously,
and any resemblance to actual persons, living or dead, business
establishments, events or locales is entirely coincidental.

This edition published by arrangement with Harlequin Books S.A.

For questions and comments about the quality of this book
please contact us at Customer_eCare@Harlequin.ca

® and TM are trademarks of the publisher. Trademarks indicated with
® are registered in the United States Patent and Trademark Office, the
Canadian Trade Marks Office and in other countries.

www.eHarlequin.com

Printed in U.S.A.

ABOUT THE AUTHOR

From the time she was ten years old and read *Anne of Green Gables* and *Little Women*, Lee McKenzie knew she wanted to be a writer, just like Anne and Jo. In the intervening years she has written everything from advertising copy to an honors thesis in paleontology, but becoming a four-time Golden Heart finalist and a Harlequin Books author are among her proudest accomplishments. Lee and her artist/teacher husband live on an island along Canada's west coast, and she loves to spend time with two of her best friends—her grown-up children.

Books by Lee McKenzie

HARLEQUIN AMERICAN ROMANCE
1167—THE MAN FOR MAGGIE
1192—WITH THIS RING
1316—FIREFIGHTER DADDY

To my dear aunt, Beverly Wegner,
for a lifetime of love and encouragement.

Your strength and courage are an inspiration. You'll
be truly missed and fondly remembered, always.

Chapter One

Strapless gowns ought to be against the law. Jess Bennett tugged at the top of hers and wished she could blend in to the decor. Not that this amount of shiny turquoise satin could merge with anything, except maybe more shiny satin. She looked around the room for the three other women who were wearing the same dress but in different colors. Nicola, in bright yellow, and her husband, Jonathan, were on the dance floor. Maria, stunning in red, was sitting with her husband, who was proudly cradling their beautiful baby daughter in his arms. Paige was... Where was Paige?

Jess's search for the fourth bridesmaid was intercepted by a man leaning against a column on the other side of the room. He was tall, and his dark good looks hinted at a Mediterranean heritage. Before now she hadn't seen him among the wedding guests, and she decided he was most likely an employee. She connected with his gaze for a second and looked away, but after failing to find her friend Paige, something drew her back to him.

He was still watching her.

She glanced down at the front of her dress and pulled it up some more. Rory, the bride, who was also one of her best friends in the world, had outfitted her bridesmaids in retro-inspired gowns that were designed to make the most of a woman's curves and cleavage. Or emphasize Jess's lack of them.

He was smiling when she looked at him again. She had a feeling he'd been watching her for a while, but he seemed more amused by her battle with the dress than he was interested in her.

Easy for him to find this funny. He was wearing an elegantly tailored suit, which probably wasn't as expensive as it looked, given what he was likely to earn working here. Meanwhile, she was decked out in a dress that was determined to abide by the laws of gravity, in spite of the torturous plastic boning stitched into the seams and an obscene amount of double-sided tape that had lost its stick sometime between the photographs and the pre-reception cocktails.

Paige, wherever she was, had the perfect figure for this kind of dress—all curvy and voluptuous. Maria, ditto. Nicola was only slightly better endowed than Jess, but nothing rattled her.

Jess debated whether to get herself a drink or go in search of Paige. Maybe both. She gave the dress a final hitch and skirted the dance floor, heading toward the bar. On the way there she waved at the bride and her adoring husband, Mitch, who were talking to two other couples. The men were probably firefighters like Mitch. Rory's vintage gown was so…her. It had a fitted bodice and a gathered tulle skirt, and instead of a veil she had opted for an elegant little white pillbox hat with netting. Jess had thought the above-the-elbow white gloves were a bit much, but Rory had said they'd be perfect and she was right.

"What will you have?" the bartender asked.

She was tempted to ask for Scotch, neat. "A glass of red wine," she said, since both the dress and the circumstances called for something a little more ladylike.

"I have cabernet and merlot, both excellent California wines."

She rested her forearms on the bar and leaned on them, shifting her weight to one foot and trying to wriggle the toes of the other. "The cabernet, I guess."

"Of course." The bartender eyed the front of her dress, and she quickly straightened.

While he poured the wine, she surveyed the bottles of Scotch lined up on a glass shelf. She should have gone with her first instinct. These were much better quality than the brands she could afford to stock at the Whiskey Sour.

"The merlot would have been a better choice," a deep male voice said over her shoulder.

She didn't have to turn around to know it was him, the man who'd been amused by her struggle with the strapless wonder. When she did turn to face him, her heart rate sped up. She had been wrong about the Mediterranean connection. His eyes were blue and he had no hint of an accent.

"You're an expert?" she asked.

He shrugged slightly. "I know a little. Would you like to dance?"

"Oh, thanks, but…" How to graciously sidestep his offer? "My feet are killing me." Which was true. "And I'm not a very good dancer." Also true.

"I am," he said. "Just follow my lead."

"But my drink—"

"It'll keep." His smile was self-assured without being overconfident, and Jess had the impression he wasn't accustomed to taking no for an answer. And before she had a chance to reinforce hers with a firm thanks-but-no-thanks, her hand was in his, and he was leading her onto the dance floor.

"Are you always this pushy?" she asked as he guided her into a simple box step.

"All I did was ask you to dance."

"And I said no."

He smiled again, a perfect smile that now held just a hint of arrogance. "And yet here you are."

His touch was light and he held her hand high as he moved them across the dance floor as gracefully as her ridiculously high-heeled shoes and lack of ability permitted. She rested her other hand on his shoulder, and she swore she could feel the dress slipping down her torso. She glanced down, relieved to see that her important parts, including the underwired push-up bra Rory had coerced her into buying, were still covered.

He lowered his head till his lips almost touched her ear. "You are too self-conscious," he said. "The dress isn't going anywhere."

He had that right. The dress was definitely not going anywhere with him. "I see your expertise with women extends beyond dancing."

He laughed, apparently unaffected by her sarcasm. "And you are a much better dancer than you let on."

Oh, please. She resisted the urge to roll her eyes.

"I'm sorry. Did that sound like a come-on? It was meant to be a compliment."

She wasn't used to getting compliments, or come-ons for that matter, so it was difficult to tell the difference. And how did he know what she was thinking?

"We should start over," he said. "My name is Michael.

The mother of the bride is a business associate of mine."

That surprised her. Rory's mother was an artist, so maybe he ran an art gallery or something. "I figured you worked here at the hotel."

His turn to be surprised. "What gave you that idea?"

"You weren't here earlier."

"Are you sure?"

Yes. I would have noticed. But he didn't need to know that. "I'm Jess," she said instead. "I'm one of Rory's bridesmaids."

Duh. As if he hadn't already figured that out.

In an abrupt move he drew her closer but only, it turned out, to maneuver them off their collision course with the bride's parents. Sam Borland and Copper Pennington were divorced—twice—but according to Rory they were back on speaking terms. Judging by the way they were gazing at each other, oblivious to everything and everyone around them, they had more than talking in mind. She was delighted for Rory, of course, but more than a little envious, too. Jess heard from her mother only when she was broke and between loser boyfriends.

Roxanne Bennett's last plea for help had been six weeks ago, and Jess had sent her two hundred of her hard-earned dollars because that was easier than putting up with a barrage of desperate phone calls. Besides, by the time Roxanne had frittered away the money, she'd have yet another loser in her life and she'd be mooching from him.

Nicola and Jonathan swung by. *Wow!* Nic mouthed after doing an approving double take when she caught a glimpse of Jess's dancing partner.

Fortunately, Michael didn't seem to notice. "Do you live in San Francisco?" he asked.

"I do. And you?"

"I'm a little north of the city, but I spend a lot of time here on business."

"I see." She wasn't used to making small talk when it wasn't required for work.

He had no trouble with it at all. "What do you do?"

"I own a little bar in the South of Market neighborhood."

That seemed to interest him more than she would have expected. "SoMa's an up-and-coming area. What's the name of your place?"

"The Whiskey Sour."

"Interesting."

But he clearly didn't think it was, and she could tell he'd never heard of it. Problem was, neither had anyone else.

"It came with the name." And a small clientele. Emphasis on small. A reality she was determined to change as soon as she scraped together enough cash or convinced the bank to lend her some so she could renovate the place.

"How long have you been in business?"

"The bar has been there since my grandfather opened it in the fifties. I took over when he died two years ago."

"I'll have to come by for a drink sometime."

"Oh. Sure, that'd be great." She could use the business, but she could not picture *this* man, wearing *this* suit, sitting in *her* bar. No one but health inspectors and bill collectors ever showed up at the Whiskey Sour wearing a suit.

She caught a glimpse of Paige and her date entering the ballroom. Hard to miss Paige's purple gown. She and Andy were holding hands. Jess smiled. Paige insisted they were just friends, but those two were so close to hooking up, it wasn't even funny.

The band stopped playing and announced they were taking a short break.

Michael let her hand go, but kept his other hand on her back.

"Thank you." A little to her surprise, she meant it. Dancing with him had been…an experience.

"The pleasure was mine. Now, let's go see about that drink of yours."

"Oh, right." She wanted to tell him she had it under control, but that persistent hand was propelling her toward the bar.

Before they got there, Rory intercepted them and linked an arm with hers. "I see you've met Michael. I need to steal my maid of honor for a few minutes," she said to him. "It's time to toss the bouquet."

"I hope you'll bring her back," he said. "I promised her a glass of wine."

"Ten minutes, tops. Then she's all yours."

Oh, please. Like she would ever be *all* his. Or anybody's. But she let Rory lead her away, reminding herself that this was the last time she had to be a bridesmaid. Unless Paige got married again—and given the way she and Andy were all over each other, that possibility was looking more likely by the minute.

Face it, Jess. If your friends don't stay married, your career as a bridesmaid could last forever. She loved these women…they were the only real family she had… but she'd be glad when they were all happily married and she could settle into being godmother and old maid Auntie Jess to everyone's kids. Those roles didn't require a reinforced bra and hazardously high heels.

"Where are we going?" she asked Rory.

"To the powder room. Until now, I haven't had a moment to chat with all of you."

Nicola, Paige and Maria were waiting for them. Maria was sitting on a chair, partially covered by a soft pink baby blanket and discreetly breastfeeding her baby girl. Finally, a practical use for a strapless gown.

Paige stood facing the mirror, and Nicola was trying to fix her hair. "What on earth were you doing to make such a mess of your updo?" she asked.

Paige didn't answer.

"There you go," Nicola said. "That's the best I can do without bobby pins and hairspray."

"She and Andy disappeared for a while," Jess said, feeling a bit mischievous. "I'm guessing they finally decided to get a room."

Paige swung around, hands on her hips. "We did not! We wanted some fresh air, so we went for walk. It's a beautiful autumn evening, but it's kind of windy."

Nicola laughed. "We must be having a hurricane. Too bad Andy didn't bring his camper. The two of you could have weathered the storm in there."

Not even Paige's professionally applied makeup could hide the deep pink flush that flashed across her face.

Maria rearranged her dress and lowered the blanket to reveal a sleeping baby. "Go easy on her, girls. She's in love. She just hasn't figured it out yet."

Paige's pink face flared red.

"I'd love to hear all the details," Rory said. "And I do mean *all* of them, but I don't want to keep everyone waiting. I just wanted to thank you gals for making my day so special. Everything's been perfect and I'm so grateful to all of you. Especially you, Jess. You've been the best maid of honor a bride could hope for."

Jess hugged her. "It's been fun." And she actually meant it. Rory's easygoing and slightly unorthodox approach to wedding planning had made the process a lot more fun than she'd expected it to be. "Did you manage to finish packing for your honeymoon?"

Excitement sparked in Rory's eyes. "We leave first thing in the morning."

"I still can't believe you're going to Disneyland," Nicola said. "And taking your stepdaughter."

The bride laughed. "It'll be perfect. Mitch said we could leave Miranda with his mother and go away on our own, but it didn't feel right. I'm not just married, I have an eight-year-old daughter. Taking a family honeymoon feels like the right thing to do, and Miranda is so excited."

Jess couldn't imagine ever meeting a man she could trust that way, never mind letting her guard down long enough to marry him, but to throw in a ready-made family on top of the bargain? No way. Not even an adorable little girl like Rory's stepdaughter. Then again, there was no chance any of this could happen to her. She hadn't even been on a date in two years, not since taking over the bar when her grandfather died. She'd been too busy working her butt off.

"I think it's wonderful," Maria said. "You're going to be such a great mom."

Paige nodded somewhat wistfully. "You already are a great mom, and you're so lucky to have such a terrific little girl."

Jess gave her a playful jab in the shoulder. "If you keep sneaking off with Andy and letting him mess up your hair like that, you might end up being a mom, too."

Everyone laughed at that, even a red-faced Paige.

Rory waved her bouquet of colorful gerbera daisies. "Okay. Time to find out who's next," she said as she herded them all into the corridor. Then she tapped Jess's shoulder. "Can we talk for a few seconds?"

"Sure. What's up?"

"Let's make sure Paige catches my bouquet."

"This is just a tradition based on some crazy superstition. Catching it doesn't guarantee a wedding." Although come to think of it, Rory had caught Nic's bouquet last fall, and look at her now.

"It's symbolic, and it definitely seems to be Paige's turn, don't you think?"

The only thing Jess knew for sure was that it wasn't hers. "How am I supposed to make sure she catches it?"

"There aren't that many single women here, and the only two you really have to watch out for are Mitch's cousins. Those two little brats have actually made a bet on which of them will snag it."

"I'll see what I can do." Although short of tackling them, she had no idea how to prevent them from being contenders.

She joined the group of single women on the small dance floor and took stock of the situation. Since there'd almost certainly be another round of wedding bells in Paige's future, it sort of did make sense to let her catch the bouquet and give everyone a chance to gush about her being the next to tie the knot. The groom's teenage twin cousins had other ideas. They had already staked out their respective territories at the front of the small group of single women and were glaring at each other.

Amateurs, Jess thought. This would be like taking candy from a couple of babies.

For a split second she allowed her attention to be diverted as she searched out the man named Michael. He was watching her, and she was surprised to feel her own competitive nature kick in. Part of her was tempted to ditch the stupid shoes, roll up her sleeves—if she had any—and grab that sucker when it sailed over Rory's shoulder. Not that she wanted to get married—far from it—but catching the bouquet would show Michael…

Show him what? She had absolutely no idea. Besides, she had agreed that Paige should catch it. So instead of going on the offensive, she positioned herself directly behind the twins.

Rory surveyed the group before turning her back on it.

Jess adopted the best linebacker stance her shoes would allow.

The band riffed a suitably dramatic tune, but the drum roll was drowned out by cheering.

In case a change to running back was necessary to get the bouquet to the intended receiver, she toed off her shoes under the dress.

With the precision of a rocket launcher, Rory propelled the bouquet over her shoulder.

Jess blocked the twins and held them out of range.

The bouquet headed straight for…oh, hell. So much for Rory's aim. It was heading straight for Jess.

She let go of one twin, reached for the stupid flowers and volleyed them in Paige's direction.

A surprised Paige fumbled the bouquet but didn't drop it, and Jess grabbed the unfettered twin before she could make a lunge for the daisies.

The bride whirled around, quickly surveyed the situation and gave her a thumbs-up.

The twins gave her a pair of matching glares.

Paige, clutching the bouquet in both hands, laughed and looked at Andy.

Gotta love it when a plan comes together. "Sorry, girls," Jess said to the irate teens. Not that she meant it. They couldn't be a day over seventeen, which meant they were way too young to even think about getting married.

Nic was in stitches. "Nice save, Jess. And nice catch," she said to Paige.

In every respect, Jess thought as she glanced from Paige's blush-pink cheeks to Andy's bewildered smile. *Very* nice catch.

Jess hiked up her full-skirted dress and stuck a foot into one of her shoes. Her toes complained vigorously. She crammed her other foot into its shoe and was hobbling off the dance floor when she spotted Michael near the bar. His gaze was still on her, and he still looked amused. Was he entertained by life in general, she wondered, or was he laughing at her? He picked up two glasses of wine and walked toward her.

I guess I'm about to find out.

He handed one of the glasses to her.

She accepted, knowing without asking that this time it was merlot.

"My money was on you catching that bouquet." So he had been laughing at her.

"It wasn't my turn." She stopped herself before

blurting out that there was no point, since she didn't have a man in her life. He didn't need to know that she had made up her mind a long time ago—at fourteen, to be exact—that it would take a very special someone to make up for the bad example set by her mother's endless string of boyfriends.

"Those shenanigans seemed to take your mind off the dress."

"What do you mean?"

"Earlier you were concerned that it would reveal too much."

He was right. For those few moments while it was her job to get the bouquet in Paige's hands, she had completely forgotten about the dress.

"So you had nothing to worry about." His gaze traveled over the top of her dress.

Sure. *Nothing* to worry about.

"I understand you're not seeing anyone."

How the hell had he figured that out? "That's a pretty big leap. Just because I didn't bring a date to the wedding doesn't mean I'm not seeing anyone."

"I'm not big on assumptions. I'd rather have facts, so I asked the mother of the bride if you were involved."

There was something surprisingly suggestive about his inference. "Involved as in…?"

"You know what I mean."

Was she supposed to be flattered that he'd gone to the trouble to find that out? "All right, then, it only seems fair that I have a few facts about you."

"What would you like to know?"

"Are you 'involved' with anyone?"

"Not at the moment." He touched her glass with his. Interesting. She was tempted to ask if he was on the rebound, but that might sound as if she had more than idle conversation in mind. Instead, she decided on a different line of questioning. "How long have you known Rory's mother?"

"Several years. We met at one of her art exhibits."

Also interesting. She was usually quick to figure out what people did for a living, and she had not pegged Michael as an artist, or even an art aficionado. "Are you in the art business?" she asked.

He hesitated before answering, which made her suspect he was hiding something.

"Business, yes," he said finally. "Not art. As it turns out, your friend Nicola's husband is also a colleague of mine."

Jonathan was a lawyer. "Do you work with him?" she asked.

"No, I'm not a lawyer. Just a client."

"One of their criminal cases?"

His laughter was genuine. "Good one. I try to stay out of trouble, or at least not get caught. Besides, Jonathan is a corporate lawyer."

Did that make Michael a corporation or just someone who worked for one? She owned her own business, but the only time she'd talked to a lawyer was when she had settled her grandfather's estate.

"You haven't tasted the wine."

Neither had he, she noticed. She obliged and took a sip. "Nice."

He looked taken aback, as though he'd expected her to say something else.

"Very nice." To emphasize her point, she took another drink.

He gave the wine in his glass a gentle swirl. "Does the Whiskey Sour have a wine list?"

"Not a list, exactly, but I do stock two kinds of wine."

"What are they?"

"Red and white."

His laugh was even sexier than his smile. "Seriously?"

Completely serious. "I really want to reinvent the place as a cocktail lounge, but right now most of my patrons are beer drinkers. A couple of my friends—Nicola and Paige, who is one of the other bridesmaids—drink wine, so I keep a few bottles on hand."

"Tasting a wine should be like a first kiss. You need to take your time and give it all your attention."

He tipped his glass slightly to one side. "Did you notice the color of this one?"

Other than it being red, she had not. She focused on the glass for a moment and wondered if she'd ever find out what a first kiss with him would be like. She looked up at him and realized he was waiting for her answer. She managed to shake her head.

He tipped his glass slightly to one side. "If the light was better, you'd see it's not red. It's a deep shade of garnet."

All she saw was a pair of dark blue eyes. "What does that mean?"

"It's well aged." He straightened his glass.

"No offense, but doesn't wine tasting strike you as being kind of pompous? I mean, they're pretty much all the same."

His only response was a stunned expression, but he recovered quickly. "Tell me something about yourself."

"Uh, what would you like to know?"

"Something I wouldn't expect to hear."

Would her wanting to explore the whole kissing thing be unexpected? Probably not. "I used to be a high school teacher and I have a brown belt in karate."

"Really? I guess that's one way to keep students in line."

She smiled at that. She wasn't cut out to be a teacher, but fortunately she'd never had to rely on the martial arts for classroom management. It had come in handy with a couple of her mother's boyfriends, though. One in particular.

Snap out of it, she told herself. She usually didn't dwell on the past, so why did it keep shoving its way into her thoughts tonight? Maybe it was being around Rory's family, or maybe it was the unexpected attention from a handsome stranger who avoided answering questions about himself, but had no trouble wheedling information out of her.

Michael swirled the contents of his glass, but he was studying her intently. "So before you taste the wine, you have to smell it." He held it out to her. "Inhale slowly, and really think about the scent."

In her book, there weren't many things more pretentious than wine tasting, but she played along and took a sniff. "It sort of smells like cherries."

He smelled it. "You're right. Ripe cherries, and just a hint of spice."

Her insides went wobbly. "Your turn. To tell me something unexpected about you, I mean."

He hesitated, as though trying to think of something that might interest her. "I'm restoring a 1954 Morgan."

Michael's hands didn't look anything like the mechanics' hands she often saw wrapped around beer mugs at the Whiskey Sour. "Are you actually doing the work yourself, or are you having it restored?"

"A little of both. You know something about cars?"

She cupped both hands around her glass. "A little. My grandfather had an old MGB. I used to help him work on it from time to time, and a lot of his friends are…were…mechanics. Some of them are still regulars at the bar."

"You should hold your glass by the stem," he said. "That way you don't transfer the warmth from your hands to the contents of the glass."

"Oh." She adjusted her hands accordingly.

"I rebuilt the engine myself. With my brother, actually. We've been working on it together. It's a nice change of pace from…what I usually do."

Okay. Maybe the brother was a mechanic.

"Now you should taste the wine again," he said, but he reached for her hand and stopped her before she could raise the glass to her lips. "Let it slide over your tongue and around the inside of your mouth before you swallow it." His voice had taken on a sinfully deep tone and she swore it was reverberating through his hand and up her arm. "Try it."

She took a sip and so did he. She watched his mouth, and didn't swallow until he did.

"What do you think?"

She was at a loss for words, and that almost never happened.

"Peppery, just a hint of oak," he said. "Full-bodied."

"Yes. You took the words right out of my mouth."

He smiled at her. "Can you still taste it?"

She thought about that for a second or two, and nodded.

"That's one of the best characteristics of this particular wine. It has a long, warm finish."

Holy crap. She should ask about his car, or his brother or what kind of business he was in. Instead she took another slow, careful sip of wine, imagined she was being kissed, and contemplated everything implied by a long, warm finish.

Chapter Two

Michael Morgan followed his real estate agent out of the shabby building she'd just shown him in the South of Market district and waited on the sidewalk while she locked the door. The large windows overlooking the street had been boarded up with plywood, and that had been covered with several coats of paint in an unsuccessful attempt to keep graffiti under control. Even the big for-sale sign had been tagged so many times, it was almost unreadable. It was the third place he'd seen and the least disastrous, which wasn't saying much.

"It definitely needs work," the agent said. "I do think it has potential, though. Nice high ceilings and all that exposed brick. And there's already lots of new development nearby." She had helped him find the two previous locations for his new wine bars—the first at Fisherman's Wharf and the second on Nob Hill—and she now had a good sense of what he wanted.

This place was a dump, but she was right, it had potential. A trendy-looking deli and coffee shop had recently opened across the street, a new residential building next door boasted upscale loft condos and there was more new construction on the next block. On the downside, this place required a major renovation and he had no idea how much of the building's character and existing structure could be salvaged, or how much capital he'd have to sink into it.

"It is a good location," he said. "Let me talk to my sister and find out when she can check it out. She's the architect who'll be handling this project."

"Of course. If it makes life easier for you, have her call me directly and we'll set up a time."

"Thanks. I'll do that." Michael unlocked his car, got in and checked his cell phone for messages. Nothing that couldn't wait. He pulled up his sister's private number and studied the building's facade while he waited for her to answer. The windows and front entrance were set in brick arches. The second-story windows were tall, almost floor-to-ceiling on the inside. He could picture them with ironwork Juliet balconies on the outside, and maybe some planters.

"Hey, big brother. What's up?"

"Hi, Lexi. I've just toured a possible location for the new wine bar in SoMa. Any chance you can take a look sometime this week?"

"I'll be happy to."

He gave her the real estate agent's number and said he'd leave it to her to set up an appointment. "I guess I'll see you at home tomorrow."

"I wouldn't miss it. What time will you be there?"

"I'm driving up first thing in the morning. I have a meeting with Ginny at the winery, then I thought I'd hang out with Ben for the rest of the day. What about you?"

"I plan to catch up on some work here and leave around lunchtime, but I'll take a look at this place before I go. The party's not till six, right?"

"That's right, but I think Mom would like you to be there a little before she serves dinner."

"Gee, you think?" Lexi laughed. "Oh, hang on a sec."

He waited and listened to her give a series of quick instructions to an assistant.

"Okay, I'm back. I've already told Mom I'll be there before dinner, and she talked me into staying the night. I also told her that if she wants us to drop everything and spend the whole day up there, then she shouldn't throw a party in the middle of the week."

He was willing to concede that Lexi made a good point, even though he didn't agree with her and neither would their mother. As far as Sophia Morgan was concerned, *nothing* was as important as family, and he felt the same way. As much as he had wanted to build on his father's business—and so far his success had exceeded even his expectations—he had done it as much for his family as for himself.

He divided his time between his family's home in Napa Valley and his apartment in San Francisco, which meant he was back and forth fairly often. His sister Ginny and her husband lived in the valley at one of the family's vineyards. Lexi was the only one who'd chosen a career outside the family business and made a permanent move to the city. She was a shrewd businesswoman, even a little hard-nosed at times, and was also the only one of his siblings who was periodically at odds with their mother. The fireworks had started the day she hit puberty, escalated through her teen years and finally settled into an accepting but arm's-length relationship around the time she left for college.

"Has our mother ever thrown a party that wasn't on the actual day of someone's birthday?" he asked.

"No, but it's not like Ben would know."

"Ah, but she would," he reminded her.

"Yeah, I know, and I'll be there. I will. Just not for the whole day."

"Okay, okay. No guilt trips from me. I'll see you sometime tomorrow afternoon."

He tossed the information packet from the Realtor into the glove compartment, took out a pair of sunglasses and flipped open his appointment book. This had been his last scheduled meeting for the day. Now he'd satisfy his curiosity about a little bar called the Whiskey Sour and the high-spirited redhead who ran the place. He'd thought a lot about both since he'd met her at Rory and Mitch's wedding on Saturday evening, and he was looking forward to seeing her again. This time on her turf.

He was more interested in her bar than he was in her, though. She had implied that her business wasn't doing all that well, so there was a very good chance she'd consider selling. And if she hadn't considered it, well, he could be persuasive.

Still, she was an intriguing woman in her own right. That amazing cascade of red hair would make any man a little crazy, and those piercing green eyes could cut through any pretense. He didn't often meet a beautiful woman who didn't use her looks to her advantage, and that's what had intrigued him most. She had introduced herself simply as Jess, but it had been easy enough to find out that her name was Jessica Bennett. She was the owner and sole proprietor of the Whiskey Sour, and according to the telephone directory she rented an apartment about six blocks away. Which might sound a bit stalkerish, but he'd learned the hard way to check out people, especially women, before letting them into his life.

Not that Jess had given any indication she wanted in. She hadn't come across as a gold digger, but then neither had most of the others. Jess seemed down-to-earth and completely unpretentious, and she had made her thoughts on wine tasting abundantly clear. She thought it was pompous. Then there'd been the quip about him being one of Jonathan's criminal cases. Somewhat to his surprise, he had found it refreshing, and it still made him smile. She might have been more restrained if she'd known who he was, but there was also a good chance she wouldn't.

The sun had finally put in an appearance, and before he drove away he put on the sunglasses and debated whether or not to put the top down. Better to leave it up, he decided. He'd have to park on the street and he wasn't all that familiar with the neighborhood. A few minutes later he pulled into a parking spot behind a red scooter and knew he'd made the right decision. Jess's bar was on the street level of a two-story building that had seen better days. It was in better shape than the place he'd just seen and although the location was sketchier, there was some new development down the block.

This should be interesting. In spite of her elegant appearance on Saturday night, she had not been comfortable in the strapless gown or the high-heeled shoes—especially not the dress—but he still had trouble picturing her running a blue-collar establishment, and that's clearly what this was.

He opened the door and stepped inside the dimly lit space, realizing he'd forgotten to leave his sunglasses

in the car. He shoved them up onto his head and waited
for his eyes to adjust. The place smelled of beer and
disinfectant with a hint of deep-fryer fat that was past
its prime. Gradually he became aware that all eyes—
those of two older men perched on stools that flanked
one corner of the bar and the young brunette behind the
bar—were on him.

Or…was that Jess?

It was. The lighting was deceptive and the brunette
was actually a redhead. He approached the bar, taking in
the unexpected transformation of the ill-at-ease woman
in the strapless blue gown into this casual ponytailed
barkeep in a man's blue-and-white-pinstriped dress shirt
worn jacket-style over a gray T-shirt. He had been oddly
attracted to the initial version, but he was out-and-out
intrigued by this one.

"This is a surprise," she said.

He'd be willing to wager that he was more surprised
than she was. Without taking her eyes off him, she finished pulling a glass of beer and slid it across the counter
to one of the only two customers in the place.

Michael nodded a greeting to the two men and took a
stool, leaving an empty one between them, and turned his
attention back to Jess. "I was in the neighborhood."

"Were you?" Her tone implied that she didn't believe
him. "What brings you down here?"

You, he was tempted to say, but that wasn't entirely
true and she'd never believe it anyway. "Real estate," he
said instead.

"I see. Buying or selling?"

"Buying."

She was back to looking skeptical again. At the wedding she had mentioned that the mechanics who had

been her grandfather's old friends still frequented the place. Her two customers had to be them.

"What can I get you?" she asked.

He thought about asking for a glass of wine just to see what she'd give him, but he was pretty sure that would tick her off. Instead, he did a quick survey of what she had on tap. A small but impressive selection. "I'll have a Guinness."

She reached for a glass and while she filled it, he studied her face. At the wedding she'd worn her hair loose and her makeup had been flawless. Today he doubted she was wearing any, except maybe some mascara. With her coloring, the long, sweeping eyelashes seemed too dark to be natural. She looked young, probably much younger than she actually was, and the faded, slim-fitting jeans and black-and-white high-topped sneakers made her seem even more youthful.

She set the glass on a cardboard coaster in front of him. "What kind of real estate are you looking for?"

"A location for a new wine bar."

"So you really do know something about wine." Her grin took the edge off the dig.

"I do."

"I sure don't need any more competition, but a wine bar sounds like the kind of place the neighborhood newbies will go for."

Unlike the two men seated at the bar. They were a couple of old-timers in every sense of the word. Michael took a quick look around the interior. "I don't know. If you fix up this place, you'd attract a diff—" The two men had stopped talking and had tuned in to his conversation with Jess. "You'd bring in more business."

She gave him a long, thoughtful look. "I'm working on it."

If she had a plan, she apparently wasn't going to share it with him. "Have you considered selling?" he asked instead.

She'd started to clean the counter with a damp cloth, but she paused in midswipe. He noticed that the pink nail polish she'd worn at the wedding was gone. "If that's why you came in here, you should have saved yourself the trouble. The Whiskey Sour is *not* for sale."

It had been an innocent enough question, but she was genuinely offended by it. "No problem. I just looked at a place on Folsom Street. It needs work, but it's the best I've seen so far." With the exception of this place. He wanted a building that had the feel of an old warehouse, in keeping with the neighborhood, and Jess's bar had everything on his list—interior brick walls, exposed overhead ducts and wiring, and original plank floors that had, over the decades, been buffed into a natural patina. Didn't she realize she was sitting on a gold mine? Then again, her business was none of his.

"Do you live around here?" Her voice sounded distant all of a sudden, and he could tell she was still suspicious about his motivation for being here. Damn. That's not what he'd intended.

"I have an apartment on Nob Hill. What about you?" he asked, although he already knew the answer.

"Not far from here." She backed away and leaned on the counter behind the bar, arms folded, ankles crossed.

This was not going well.

He took the sunglasses off his head, folded them and set them on the bar. "So I was wondering, would you like to go out for dinner sometime?" She looked as surprised as he felt. He'd thought a lot about asking her out since he'd danced with her on Saturday night, but he usually had more finesse than this.

"Oh. Um…I work here most nights so…no. But thanks."

The skinny man sitting closest to him shifted slightly on his stool. "She doesn't work on Thursdays," he said.

"Larry! No help from the peanut gallery."

Both men were smiling broadly and nudging one another with their elbows. "When was the last time you went out on a date?" the heavyset man asked.

Jess's face turned a revealing shade of red. "Bill, that goes for you, too. You guys are as bad as Granddad used to be."

The man named Larry wasn't finished. "She has another bartender who's here every Thursday," he said to Michael. "So tomorrow night would be good."

Michael laughed. He felt a bit like a teenager asking a girl's father for permission to take her out. "Thursdays. Good to know. Unfortunately, I have plans tomorrow. A family dinner," he added quickly so she didn't think it was a date. "It's my brother's birthday. Next Thursday would be good, though." He hoped he was free that night, but if there was something on his calendar, it would be easy enough to change.

Jess stepped forward, planted both hands flat on the bartop and leaned toward him. "Hello? I said no."

Ah, but did she mean it? He put his own hand down so it was almost touching hers. "I'd be interested to hear your thoughts on running a bar in this part of the city. It would just be a business dinner."

"A *free* business dinner," Larry said.

Bill, who'd been slowly nursing his beer, set his glass down. "Never look a gift horse in the mouth."

Jess rolled her eyes and glared at them.

Michael was sure she was having second thoughts.

"Do you have a pen?" he asked.

She plucked one from a jar beside the cash register and handed it to him.

"Thanks." He took a fresh coaster from a stack on the bar, flipped it over and wrote his number on the back. "This is my cell phone. I'll pick you up here at six next Thursday, but if something comes up you can call me." He could give her a business card but decided against it. Too much information. For a second he had even debated whether or not to write his last name on the coaster, but he left it at Michael. Until he got to know her, the less she knew about him, the better.

He slid the coaster across the bar. She didn't pick it up, but he knew she'd keep it, and although she still hadn't said yes, she had stopped saying no.

He swiveled a little to the right on the wobbly seat of the bar stool. "You gentlemen must be regulars," he said to Larry and Bill.

As he had surmised, both were mechanics who worked nearby. They'd been dropping in for a beer every day after work for years, had been longtime friends of Jess's grandfather and had more or less watched her grow up, which accounted for their avuncular affection. They talked about cars and he told them about the old Morgan he and his brother were restoring while he drank his Guinness and subtly—at least he hoped he was being subtle—watched the woman behind the bar.

Likewise, Jess kept herself busy, but he could tell she

didn't miss a beat. She perked up when their talk drifted
to the old sports car he was restoring. He thought she
might even join their conversation, but she didn't. Larry
said he knew of a reliable supplier for rebuilt auto parts.
Michael pocketed the man's card and said he'd be sure
to give him a call when he needed something.

Twenty minutes later, after he finished his beer, he
pulled out his wallet and opened it. Before he withdrew
a bill, he finally made eye contact with Jess. "Walk me
out?" he asked.

He half expected her to tell him to get lost, but she
skirted the bar and joined him. He tossed a bill onto the
counter and walked with her to the door. He wanted to
touch her, but he knew she wouldn't want that, not with
Larry and Bill watching.

"I enjoyed meeting your friends at the wedding," he
said instead. "You and Rory and the other bridesmaids
seem pretty tight."

"We are. They're like my family. Now that my granddad's gone, they're really the only family I have."

Interesting. He couldn't imagine life without a close-
knit family—a biological one—and was tempted to ask
about her parents. No, that could wait. She gave the
impression she would open up only when she was ready
and not a moment sooner.

"Having friends who have your back is always a good
thing." He pushed the door open and she followed him
outside. "So I'll see you next Thursday."

She drew the front of her shirt closed and folded her
arms over it. "No offence, but why do you want to go out
with me? The woman you met at the wedding the other
night isn't the real me. This—" she uncrossed her arms
and made a sweeping gesture "—*this* is the real me."

"Relax. It's business, and it's just dinner. I'm interested to hear what you think of my plan for the new wine bar." Which wasn't the case at all. Once he made up his mind about something—and he already knew what he wanted in this neighborhood—he wasn't interested in what anyone else had to say about it. He had good instincts about these things and so far following them had paid off.

"So long as we're clear about one thing. Dinner is strictly business, and the Whiskey Sour is *not* for sale."

Or so she thought. Everything and everybody had a price. He could be very persuasive, and he was accustomed to getting what he wanted. And right now he wanted the Whiskey Sour. "Understood. I'd like to hear what you have planned for this place, too." He had the impression that she didn't actually have a plan, though, and that was going to work to his advantage. "See you next week."

"Sure. But really—" She was back to looking like a deer in the headlights.

"No buts." He opened his car door, and there was no missing the upward arch of her eyebrows. "See you next week."

Chapter Three

Jess stood by the door, watching Michael slide behind the wheel of his Boxster and drive away. Wow. That was some car. Jet-black with tan upholstery. Wine bars must be more lucrative than seedy little taverns. All she could afford was a secondhand Vespa.

After he disappeared around the corner, she went back inside. Larry and Bill were just finishing their second round, which meant they'd be leaving soon. Both were sporting ear-to-ear grins.

"Do *not* start with me," she warned them.

"Wouldn't dream of it," Larry said. He leaned sideways and slid the money Michael had left toward her.

Twenty bucks for a $5.95 glass of beer. Was he always this generous or did he feel sorry for her?

"Big tipper," he said.

Jess rang in the sale, grabbed the bill off the counter and stuffed it into the cash drawer.

Larry reached for a coaster—the one with Michael's phone number—and slid that toward her. "Better put this away for safekeeping, too."

"I said don't start."

Bill laughed, a big booming laugh in keeping with his

size. "He forgot his sunglasses, too. Maybe you ought to call that number and let him know."

Sure enough, Michael's glasses sat on the bar next to his empty glass. Had he left them behind on purpose? Maybe an excuse to come back or, as Bill was suggesting, a way to get her to call him. No, that didn't seem like his style. He sure hadn't needed a reason to show up this afternoon. It was obvious that he'd come here looking for a piece of SoMa real estate, and he could damn well think again. She loved this place. It was the only thing in her life that had any real significance, and she no intention of selling.

To her annoyance, though, she had thought about Michael a lot since Saturday night. She had even debated whether or not to ask Rory for the scoop on him when she got back from her honeymoon. Or she could ask Nic to find out what kind of legal work Jonathan did for him. But what would be the point? Sure, she was curious, but she hadn't actually expected to see him again. Besides, if either of them told him that she was fishing for information, he might get the wrong idea.

She picked up the sunglasses and pulled the lost-and-found box from under the counter. The box contained two gloves that didn't match, a cigarette lighter with an ornate letter *P* engraved on it, a tube of red lipstick, a couple of stray keys, several unpaired earrings and a tacky little gold vinyl change purse that contained eighty-seven cents. A bunch of crap no one would ever claim but that she couldn't bring herself to throw out. The gold logo on the arm of Michael's glasses indicated that they were neither cheap nor trashy. She slid the box back into place and set the sunglasses on the counter at the back of the bar. No way would she use them as an excuse to call him. If he didn't come back for them, and she had a pretty good hunch he wouldn't, she could give them to him when he picked her up next week.

Larry drained his glass and set it on the bar. "I'd best be getting home to the missus. She'll have dinner on the table pretty soon."

"Or you could take the missus out for dinner," Bill said. "I hear the ladies like that sort of thing."

Bill had been a confirmed bachelor for as long as she'd known him, which was pretty much forever. She also knew neither of them would let this go unless she played along with them, so she leaned on the counter and struck the phoniest dreamy-eyed schoolgirl pose she could muster. "Us gals are *totally* into being wined and dined." She tipped her head to one side and batted her lashes. *"Totally."*

They laughed and she joined in while they paid for their drinks. She was not the wine-me, dine-me type at all, and her friends knew it.

"Wish I could afford to give you a big tip," Larry said.

"I don't expect tips from you guys," she said. "I just appreciate your business." She appreciated their loyalty even more.

Both glanced surreptitiously at the room full of empty tables.

"No worries. Things will pick up a little later," she said. "They always do."

They knew as well as she did that was often not the case, but they were too polite to say it. She had tried all kinds of things to bring in new patrons—everything from putting leaflets on the windshields of parked cars in the area to a speed-dating night. The leaflets had ended up littering the sidewalk and the speed-dating thing had been an unmitigated disaster. The place needed a serious facelift and she could swing that only if her application for a bank loan was approved. The guy at the bank had done some serious eyebrows hikes when he'd assessed her financial situation, then said he'd get back to her in a few weeks. All she could do now was wait and see.

Bill pushed the door open and slid a ball cap onto his head. "'Night, Jess."

Larry waved. "You take care, girl."

"For sure. Good night, guys. I guess I'll see you Friday." She usually dropped in on Thursday even though it was her night off, but Paige was moving into a new apartment and Jess had promised to help her pack.

After they left she picked up the coaster that had Michael's number on it, and it dawned on her that she didn't even know his last name. She put the coaster under the tray in the cash drawer and reached for his sunglasses. The next thing she knew, she had them on. She looked at herself in the mirror behind the rows of bottles.

"What the hell are you doing?" She whipped them off again. "Mooning around over some guy who'll probably turn out to be a total jerk."

When it came to men, she had lousy luck, and she blamed that on her mother. Roxanne Bennett was a slut, no two ways about it. She had a habit of hooking up with losers who didn't give a damn about her or her daughter, and Jess's father had been one of them. There'd been countless nights when Jess heard her mother stumble in after the bars closed, laughing and shushing some loudmouthed guy, telling him not to wake up her kid. And the morning after, how many times had a strange man caught her off guard in the kitchen and scared the crap out of her while she was making peanut butter sandwiches—one for breakfast and another for lunch—and hoping to sneak out to school before her mother and the creep du jour woke up?

"Stop it," she said to her reflection. The past was the past. With her granddad's help she'd put it behind her a long time ago, and the best way to keep it in the past was to not let herself think about it.

Michael was nothing like the men her mother had dragged into their lives, but he was very sure of himself, cocky even, and clearly successful. He was the kind of man who liked getting what he wanted, and she had a feeling he wanted her bar.

Still, she was going out for dinner with one of the sexiest men she had ever met. One of? He could be a contender for *the* sexiest man alive. A man who was going to pick her up next week in that flashy car of his and take her out to dinner to discuss business, and she had absolutely nothing to wear. For the first time in her life she wished she had a clue about what kind of clothes a woman wore to a business dinner with a man who drove a Porsche and wore designer shades.

Rory had enough fashion sense for both of them, but she was on her honeymoon, and Nicola's expensive tastes would put her in the poorhouse. Jess reached for the phone and punched in Paige's number. She was up to her eyeballs in packing boxes but this was a fashion nine-one-one call, after all, and there was a first time for everything. Paige would understand.

To BEAT THE MORNING rush hour, Michael got up at dawn and drove through the still-slumbering city and north across the Golden Gate. That morning the bridge and the bay were frosted with a thick layer of fog, but a quick glance over his shoulder showed the lights of the city still sparkled against the lightening sky. He'd made this hour-and-a-half commute more times than he could count, but he never tired of the scenery, especially at sunrise. Now with the city behind him, he looked forward to going home.

For the past few years, business had drawn him into the city more and more frequently and he had finally rented an apartment in Nob Hill so he had a home base. Or at least a place to stay and a place to entertain business colleagues as often as required. The plan had been to buy a condo or a town house, but he hadn't found the time or the need to get that settled. Living in the city had taken some getting used to, but now he appreciated the noise and chaotic confusion as much as he cherished the order and symmetry of the countryside and vineyards that had been his backyard since childhood.

In a couple of hours the roads would be busy with the tour buses that were the bread and butter for many of the smaller wineries and still a welcome addition to the bigger enterprises like Morgan Estate. As his car made quick work of the miles, he took in the sprawling, linear vineyards and tried to run through a mental inventory of everything he needed to cover at his meetings that morning, but his mind kept drifting to dinner with Jess next week.

Where should he take her? Most of the women he'd dated preferred someplace elegant and expensive, but he could tell that wasn't her style. They could drive up here to the valley—he knew of several out-of-the-way places—but it was too soon for that, he decided. Besides, this was a business dinner, not a date.

He could take her to his wine bar at Fisherman's Wharf, or they could stay in SoMa. Come to think of it…maybe they should do both. He smiled and tapped his fingers on the steering wheel. He had an idea that just might work, in more ways than one.

The sun was well up by the time he arrived at the house and he looked forward to joining his family for breakfast. Instead of driving into his space in the garage, he pulled up on the cobblestone roundabout by the front entrance and popped the trunk. He slung the leather strap of his briefcase over his shoulder, took out the big, bright, professionally wrapped package and slammed the trunk shut.

Right on cue, the front door flew open.

"Mikey! Mikey!" His brother had given him the childish nickname years ago and continued to use it because he'd never been able to wrap his tongue around the *L* in Michael.

"Hey, Ben. What are you up to this morning?" This adult-sized child's soft, round features and ear-to-ear grin never failed to bring out Michael's protective instincts.

"Fix my car today?" Ben asked.

"We're not going to work on the car today, sport," he said, more than happy to let his brother take ownership of a car he would someday be able to ride in but would never be able to drive. "It's your birthday, remember?"

Ben reached for the gift, the pudgy fingers of both hands splayed. "My present?"

"It sure is, but you have to wait till your party to open it."

"Open it now!"

Too late, Michael realized he should have left the gift in the trunk until Ben was otherwise occupied. "Where's Poppy?" he asked.

The diversion tactic worked. Ben spun around and ran into the house as fast as his stocky legs would carry him, yelling, "Pop! Pop! Poppy!"

"Honey, why are you shouting?" Their mother's calm, melodic voice drifted through the house.

"Mikey's home! Where's Poppy?"

"Michael? Are you here already?"

"Yes, I am," he called to her. "I'll be right there." He nudged open the door to his father's den off the foyer, stashed Ben's gift in a cabinet and set his briefcase on the floor next to the desk. He didn't think of this room as his office, although it's where he worked when he was here. He could still picture his father sitting in one of the big, coffee-colored leather armchairs by the gas fireplace, reading, and he could even detect the faint smell of pipe tobacco. It had been the only room in the house where his father smoked. After eight years, Michael wasn't sure if the scent still lingered in the room or just in his memory.

He left the den and followed his nose to the kitchen.

"You're earlier than usual." His mother reached up and gave him a hug, then presented one lightly powdered cheek for a kiss. She was one of those rare women who appeared in the kitchen first thing in the morning fully dressed, hair done and makeup applied, long before anyone else in the family was awake.

"I'm meeting with Ginny this morning, then I have

a working lunch with Drew Attwell at the winery. That should wrap up by two at the latest, and then I'll come back and spend the rest of the afternoon with Ben."

"Thank you. He's been asking about you every five minutes. I haven't seen Drew in a while. How's he doing these days?"

"Working as hard as ever. He's the best winemaker in the valley, in my opinion, and I don't think you'll find many people who'll disagree." He picked up a fresh scone, still warm from the oven, broke it in half and inhaled the scent of finely grated orange peel. "Smells delicious. I was counting on being here in time for breakfast."

She smiled up at him. "I thought you might be. That's why I baked them."

His mother's scones were the best in the world, bar none. "Thanks. These are delicious, as always."

"Vanessa didn't come up with you?"

This was bound to come up sooner or later, so he might as well get it over with. "We're not seeing each other anymore."

Sophia had started to load the dishwasher, but she stopped and gave him one of her intense stares. "I'm sorry to hear that. What happened?"

"She's looking for greener pastures." As in the color-of-money green.

"Hard to imagine her finding a better catch than you."

And Vanessa had seen him as exactly that—a good catch. It hadn't taken him long to realize their relationship was going nowhere, and if he hadn't been so preoccupied with business he would have broken things off himself. Better that she'd been the one to end it, though. Fewer hard feelings on her part and none on his.

"She was looking for an engagement ring," he said. The bigger and more expensive, the better. Problem was, he was *not* in the market for a trophy wife. "I didn't give her one."

"Michael, you're thirty-seven. I know you have a good life, but I would like to see you settled with a wife and family."

With an emphasis on family. Sophia Morgan was extremely proud of her children's accomplishments and at the same time intensely disappointed that so far not one of them had produced a grandchild. She reminded them of that shortcoming every chance she got.

"It'll happen when it happens, Mom." Just not with a gold digger like Vanessa.

Jess, by comparison, struck him as a woman with a mind of her own and an unwillingness to settle for being anybody's trophy wife, although she was certainly stunning enough to pass for one, even in a well-worn pair of blue jeans and a baggy man's shirt. There'd never been a shortage of women for him to take to dinner, but it had been ages since he'd been in such a hurry to invite one to join him. He was looking forward to next Thursday, and he had a hunch Jess was, too, if for no other reason than to satisfy her curiosity about him and check out the latest competition for the Whiskey Sour.

"So, any prospects?" his mother asked.

"Not so far." There was no point in telling her about Jess, because the tiny, insignificant detail of them not yet having had a first date would not stop from her from daydreaming about bridal registries and grandbabies.

"Poppy!" Ben had flung open the French doors off

the breakfast room and an energetic little ball of white fluff tore through the kitchen and tackled Michael's shoe.

Michael scooped the little dog into his arms. "How is she?" he asked Ben.

"She poops on the lawn."

Sophia ignored her youngest child's lack of discretion and poured a cup of coffee for Michael. "The lawn is a vast improvement over the carpet in the family room," she said in a droll voice.

He picked up the coffee cup, laughing. "Thanks, Mom."

The little bichon frise had been Ben's birthday gift from the family last year. He called her Poppy because she had looked like an oversize kernel of popcorn, which happened to be his favorite food, and it was an easy word for him to say. He had gone through a worrisome period of leth argy that had puzzled the doctors and troubled the family. They'd tried everything to coax him out of it, but nothing worked. Nothing, until Poppy had come into his life. His mother had reluctantly agreed to the dog, in part because she'd been so worried about Ben and also because Ginny and her husband had promised to take it if it didn't work out with Ben. They had hoped that having a dog would help to keep him active, and it had paid off.

"Have you been taking her for a walk every day?" he asked his brother.

Ben's head bobbed enthusiastically. "Two times." He held up one hand and displayed all five digits, then tried to cover several of them with the other hand.

"We walk her through the vineyard twice a day,"

their mother said. "Every morning and again before dinner."

Michael tousled his brother's hair. "Good job, Ben."

Ben beamed.

"Lexi called last night. She said she has to work today." His mother gave him an admonishing look. "She said she'll drive up in time for Ben's birthday dinner tonight."

Michael set a squirming Poppy on the floor. "It's not my fault she's working all day. I asked her to take a look at a property I'm interested in, but she didn't have to do it today."

"You knew very well she wouldn't postpone something like that."

True. Neither would he. He appreciated Lexi's prompt attention to this, since this latest prospect was the best he'd seen so far. Tonight he would find time to have a private talk with her about checking out the Whiskey Sour—surreptitiously, of course—because he was becoming convinced that he should hold off making an offer on the other location until he'd had dinner with Jess. Her place needed a lot less work and could be open for business much sooner than the dump he'd seen yesterday. That meant he could even sweeten the deal for Jess and it would be a win-win situation for both of them. She'd been pretty adamant about not selling, but money had a way of changing people's minds.

"You and Lexi are both cursed with the Morgan workaholic gene."

As far as he was concerned, not putting off till tomorrow what could be done today hardly made him a workaholic, and it sure didn't seem like a curse. In the eight years since his father had passed away, he had taken Morgan Estate Winery from a small family-owned-and-operated cottage industry to a large, successful company with numerous vineyards throughout the Napa Valley, and now an expanding chain of wine bars in San Francisco.

"What are you and Ginny up to this morning?"

"She's wrapping up the marketing campaign for the new pinot noir we're releasing this fall and wants me to take a look at it."

"Ginny shouldn't be working at all. It's only been two months since she was—" His mother paused and glanced at Ben, who was watching television in the family room. "Since she was in the hospital."

Michael sighed. His sister wasn't sick, she'd had a miscarriage a month ago and she seemed to be doing fine. "Ginny's the most conscientious person I know. She wouldn't be working if her doctor hadn't green-lighted her."

"She might be fine physically, but she's still emotionally vulnerable."

"Then keeping busy is probably good for her." He covered one of his mother's hands with both of his. "It's what you would do."

He could tell from her reaction that he was right and she knew it.

"I know you want to protect us and make everything perfect, but we're all capable, responsible adults."

She cast another look at Ben, but this time her eyes were filled with love and just a hint of longing for something that would never be.

He knew what she was thinking. *All of you except Ben.*

He knew she worried about his future, about what

would happen to him when the day came that she couldn't look after him. Michael and his sisters had made a commitment to continue contributing to the trust fund their father had set up for Ben, but that's not what concerned Sophia Morgan. Since no one knew Ben the way she did, no one could possibly love him as much as she did. Which wasn't true—Michael and his sisters doted on their little brother, even though they'd never talked about who would look after him if their mother couldn't. Partly because no one was ready to accept the reality that their mother wasn't getting any younger and partly because each secretly hoped one of the others would step up and take on the responsibility.

Ben abandoned the television and wandered back to the kitchen.

"Would you like a scone?" Sophia asked.

"Juice."

"Juice, please."

Ben gave her an eager nod.

"Can you say it?"

"Yup. Juice *puh-leeeeez.*"

"Good boy. Sit with Michael and I'll get it for you."

Ben settled into the next chair. "Mikey wants juice?"

"No, thanks. I'll stick with coffee."

"Don't like coffee," Ben said. "Like juice." As soon as his mother set the glass of orange juice in front of him, he grabbed it and took a gulp. "See? Mustache!" he said, pointing to his upper lip.

Sophia handed him a napkin.

Michael laughed. "I see that."

"We'll fix the car?"

"Not today," Michael reminded him. "I'm going to see Aunt Ginny this morning."

"Ginny's baby got lost. Me 'n' Poppy are looking for it."

"Are you? Ginny must be happy about that."

"Yup. Dogs are good at finding people."

"They sure are."

"What time did you say you'd be back?" his mother asked. She looked more tired than usual and he wondered if she was feeling all right.

"I should be back here by two o'clock."

Ben drained his glass and set it on the table with a loud thunk. "Then we'll fix the car?"

"Not today. But I met a mechanic in the city yesterday, and he's going to help me find some of the parts we need. As soon as we get those, we'll fix it. Okay?"

"Okay."

"How about we take Poppy for a walk this afternoon?" He had thought that would free up some of Sophia's time to work on the birthday dinner preparations, and her look of gratitude told him he was right. He was happy to do that for her, just as he was happy to spend the time with Ben, and it had been months since he'd walked through the vineyard here at the house.

"Go for a walk an' look for the baby."

"Good idea." He could see that his mother was losing patience with Ben's repeated references to the missing baby, but it was his way of processing information. Sophia had decided it best not to try to explain the miscarriage to him and that had probably been a good idea, but he had overheard her say that Ginny had lost the baby, and he had taken it literally. Ben's preoccupation with the missing infant would last until something else out of the ordinary captured his attention.

Sophia Morgan's impatience was uncharacteristic, though, which caused him another little niggle of concern. He and his sisters tended to take her for granted, but she wasn't getting any younger. If looking after the house and Ben and the dog were becoming too much for her, then they needed to find a solution. Since none of them were in a position to take on the responsibility of caring for Ben, it was time they looked into hiring someone who could. He watched the way his mother efficiently organized baking pans and utensils and the ingredients for Ben's birthday cake, and dreaded the day he'd have to break *that* news to her.

Chapter Four

After Ben's birthday dinner, Michael stood on the terrace outside the French doors, listening to the stillness and enjoying a few moments of solitude while waiting for Poppy to do her business and come back inside for the night. Ginny and Paul had gone home and Lexi was putting away the last load from the dishwasher. Like all of Sophia Morgan's dinner parties, this one had been a triumphant success. Now the birthday boy was upstairs getting ready for bed, with his mother's help, of course. It was something Ben should be doing by himself, but Sophia had been babying him for twenty-one years and she wasn't about to stop. When the time came to hire a caregiver for Ben, this would make finding someone suitable that much harder.

Michael whistled softly when the little white dog disappeared beneath some shrubs. She reappeared and raced across the lawn, a flash of white hurtling in his direction. "Time to come in, you little rascal."

Inside the house, she tore through the family room toward the kitchen, leaping and jumping around Lexi's legs.

"Get down!" She finished stacking clean dinner plates on the counter and closed the dishwasher. "This dog has no manners at all." But much as she tried to feign indifference toward Poppy, Michael had caught her sneaking tidbits of food off her plate and feeding them to the little dog that sat eagerly under her chair. He also knew she'd leave her bedroom door ajar when she went to bed, with the hope that Poppy might find her way in there.

Carefully hidden beneath Lexi's tough, no-nonsense exterior was a soft heart and a generous spirit that few people ever got to see. She had always been the studious one in the family, bookish, really, with an artistic flair. While Ginny tended to be a little flamboyant at times, Lexi had a quieter, more casual elegance about her. Ginny was all laughter and warm hugs and put family first. Lexi was more reserved and 100 percent committed to her career. At thirty-one she was already one of San Francisco's up-and-coming architects. It wasn't that she didn't care about the family, Poppy included. She just didn't wear her heart on her sleeve.

"How about another glass of wine?" he asked. "Neither of us has to drive anywhere tonight."

"You know what I'd really like?"

"Gee, let me guess."

She grinned. "A beer."

Three generations of Morgans in the wine-making business had not rubbed off on her. "Mom always keeps some in the fridge. Help yourself."

He got her a glass from the cabinet on the other side of the kitchen and uncorked a bottle of the pinot noir they'd had with dinner—the new wine they were getting ready to release and the focus of Ginny's latest marketing campaign. It was one of the finest he'd tasted in a good long while, and definitely Morgan Estate's best pinot noir yet. Elegant, smooth and complex.

He and Lexi carried their drinks into the den. She curled up in one of the big leather armchairs and tucked her feet under her.

The room felt cool, so Michael flipped the switch to turn on the gas fireplace, then took the other chair and lifted his feet onto the ottoman. They held up their glasses and touched one to the other. "Cheers," they said unison.

He held up his glass to the firelight and studied the contents. "What did you think of the new wine? You didn't say anything about it during dinner."

"I liked it. Aroma of black cherry and raspberry with a hint of floral. Soft tannins, balanced flavors of ripe cherries with a touch of spice. Medium finish with a subtle earthiness," she said, carefully repeating everything he and Ginny had said as they'd introduced it to the family.

He laughed at that. "Good to know you were paying attention."

"Seriously, I do like it. It's a lot mellower than the merlot you released earlier this year."

Her mention of that particular wine, which happened to be one of his all-time favorites, reminded him of Jess's wine-tasting tutorial at the wedding reception. She probably would have preferred beer, too.

"What are you smiling about?" Lexi asked.

"Nothing," he said quickly. He definitely wanted to talk to her about Jess, just not about last Saturday evening. "I was just thinking Mom threw a great party tonight."

"She always does, and your gift was a big hit."

"I knew it would be." He had searched online and found a model of a 1954 Morgan like the one their father had bought but never got around to restoring—the car he and Ben were now working on. Ben loved that car, and he had proudly carried the model up to his bedroom tonight, declaring his intention to sleep with it. Changing his mind would require a great deal of patience and some creative alternative suggestions from their mother.

"How did Mom seem to you tonight?"

"Same as ever. Organized and totally in control. Formidable. Why?"

"When I got here this morning she looked kind of tired—worn-out, actually."

"You worry too much. She seems fine to me."

Lexi was probably right. Ginny had said much the same thing when he'd asked her, and she spent more time with their mother than either he or Lexi did, so he should trust her judgment. Especially since he had more pressing matters on his mind.

"So you had a chance to take a look at the building I saw this week. What did you think?" He'd been itching to ask since the moment she arrived, but their mother had one rule about discussing business during dinner. It was strictly forbidden. Dinnertime was family time, no exceptions.

"I spent a couple of hours there this afternoon and gave the place a pretty good going over."

"And?"

"I have to tell you, Michael, it needs *a lot* of work. New wiring for sure, and the plumbing is way below standard. It might need a seismic upgrade, too, but that's outside my area of expertise. We'll have to bring in an engineer to be sure."

If that was the case, he would have to seriously re-think the budget for this project. "Do you think it's a good investment?"

"Right now? In that part of the city? Definitely. Of course, how good an investment will depend on how much money you're prepared to put into it."

"I've been thinking the same thing." He sipped his wine thoughtfully. He'd also been thinking that a building in better shape would be an even better investment.

"I have some ideas about how to maximize the main-floor space, and I'll give some more thought to the of-fices on the second floor. If you still plan to lease that space upstairs, you can get away with something fairly generic. That'll save you a few bucks."

"I'm looking forward to seeing what you have in mind." She had been right on the money with the first two wine bars, and he was confident she'd do the same with this location.

"I ran out of time this afternoon, so I'll go back on Saturday and check out a few more things. After that, I'll write up a preliminary report and get it to you by Monday, Tuesday at the latest. How does that sound?"

"Makes me glad you're part of the family." And he meant it. "While you're at it, can I ask another favor?"

"*Another* favor? Gee, you'd almost think you're the one who paid my college tuition and helped me set up a business."

She always adopted that pseudosarcastic tone to cover up her gratitude, and as usual he wasn't buying it. "Come on, Lex. *I* didn't pay for it, the *family* did." None of this was just about him, especially not the money.

"Yeah, yeah. So what's the favor?"

"I'd like you to check out another building a couple of blocks away. Similar in size and age, I think, but in much better shape."

"What's the asking price? I can already tell you that if it's in the same ballpark, you'd be *way* further ahead."

"About that…there's a bit of a hitch."

"What's that?"

"It's technically not for sale."

Her glass paused on its way to her mouth. "I see. That's *a bit of a hitch,* all right. Is it vacant?"

"No. Right now it's a grungy little bar called the Whiskey Sour."

"Sounds like something out of the fifties. In a good way, I suppose." She laughed, took a drink and set the glass on the small table between them.

"I gather it was a going concern in its heyday."

"And now?"

He shrugged. "Not so much. Seems to be a hangout for some of the locals. Mechanics, warehouse workers."

"A blue-collar joint isn't your usual hangout. How did you happen upon the Whiskey Sour?"

He had nothing to hide. "I met the owner at a wedding."

She was studying him like a textbook. "Who got married?"

"Remember the artist we commissioned to do the paintings for the wine bar at Fisherman's Wharf? Her daughter got married and I got an invitation."

Lexi's scrutiny intensified. "And you went?"

Of course he'd gone. The bride's mother was a well-known artist, her father was a bestselling author, the guest list was equally impressive, and that added up to a lot of potential business contacts. Instead of explaining that to Lexi, he decided to have some fun with her instead. "Why wouldn't I go? Weddings are great places to meet women. Everyone knows that."

She picked up her glass, took a mouthful and swallowed slowly without taking her eyes off him. "Interesting."

"What does that mean?"

"It means I'm not surprised you met a woman—they throw themselves at you all the time—but to have the good fortune to meet one who happens to own a bar that isn't doing so well, in the area where you just happen to be in the market for a bar. Nice work."

Jess had definitely *not* thrown herself at him. The opposite, in fact. But Lexi didn't need to know it had taken all his powers of persuasion just to get her on the dance floor. "She was one of the bridesmaids and she didn't have a date, so I asked her to dance."

Lexi rolled her eyes.

"I was doing her a favor," he said, knowing she wouldn't take him seriously. "No one wants to see a beautiful woman turn into a wallflower."

"And they say chivalry is dead. Shows you what *they* know."

"Very funny. And for the record, finding out she owns a bar in that neighborhood was a complete coincidence. I swear."

"Hey, I believe you. But even though it's not for sale, you still want me to take a look at it? This makes me think that you, dear brother, are working on a plan to sweet-talk this *beautiful* woman into selling the place to you."

"By the sound of things, I'll be doing her a favor." After seeing the place, he was sure of it. "She inherited it and I get the impression she doesn't know much about running a business. We're meeting next week to talk about it."

Lexi uncurled her legs and stretched them toward the fire. "Mmm, nice. So, does the woman know it's a meeting or does she think it's a date?"

Few people could make him squirm the way Lexi could. "She knows I'm looking for a location for a wine bar. And if you must know, she said no to going to dinner with me until I told her it was just a business meeting."

"She said no? To you? That's interesting. What's this woman's name?"

"Jess Bennett. Why?"

"If I'm going to drop by and see her, I should know who to ask for."

Okay, maybe this wasn't such a good idea. "I don't want you to go in there and actually *talk* to her. Just have a look around and let me know what you think."

She laughed. "Are you sure it's just the building you're after?"

Here we go, he thought. "Just the building. Is that so hard to believe?"

She gazed thoughtfully into the fire. "Coming from you? Mr. Emotionally Unavailable? I guess not. You always date fashionista divas like Vanessa, so the proprietor of a 'grungy' blue-collar bar doesn't fit the mold."

Ouch. Lexi's assessment made him sound superficial,

but he didn't see it that way. He had a full life and a busy one, and dating women like Vanessa was easy and uncomplicated because there was no danger of forming any attachments. Along with being a gold digger, she was also a clotheshorse with very expensive tastes. The woman before her had a thing for flashy imports. God, how many times had she gushed about how much she wanted to slap a personalized plate on one? More times than he'd bothered to count. And before her? Ah, yes. The diamonds-are-a-girl's-best-friend girl.

Lexi was right about one thing, though. He had a consistent track record. One mold, multiple casts. They were easy women to find, and when he asked them out they never said no. He knew better than to fall for them, and especially not to give them everything their little hearts desired. His first serious girlfriend had sweet-talked him into a Lexus and an engagement ring, which had still been on her finger the day she'd driven out of his life. The only thing she'd left behind was a maxed-out credit card.

Jess was uncomfortable in an evening gown, she wore old jeans and high-tops to work and if she'd been wearing any jewelry on either occasion, it hadn't made an impression on him. If her taste in cars was anything like her taste in wine, she most likely drove an old clunker. She was unpretentious, feisty and far more beautiful than she knew. Based on his experience, one of a kind. After Jess, they'd broken the mold.

He looked away from the fire and met Lexi's gaze. "When you go into the Whiskey Sour, you'll be discreet? I'd really appreciate it if you don't let on who you are or why you're there."

"No fear. They'll call me Bond." She struck a

dramatic pose, head turned to one side and eyes narrowed. "James Bond."

They both laughed. When he got too intense, he could always count on her to put things back in perspective. "On the plus side, you can order a beer while you're there," he quipped. "Who knows, you might even like the place."

"Ha-ha." She picked up her glass, angled it in his direction and then drained the last few mouthfuls. "I'm going to turn in. I have to be on the road by seven or I'll be late getting to the office. What about you?"

"I have another meeting with Ginny in the morning. I'll take Ben and Poppy for a walk so Mom can have a break, and then I'll head back after lunch."

"You're a good son," she said with a wink. "No wonder she likes you best."

He laughed. Sophia Morgan didn't play favorites and she never had, not even when Lexi's hormonal teen years had made loving her a challenge. "Good night, Lex. If you see Mom upstairs, you can tell her I'll lock up."

"Will do." Lexi stood and worked the kinks out of her legs. On her way out of the study she circled around the back of his chair and wound her arms around his neck. "Good night, big brother. See you in the morning." She paused in the doorway. "Sorry for the 'emotionally unavailable' remark. You know I wasn't serious."

"Yes, you were." And she was right. He was, but he didn't see the need to apologize for it.

"Yeah, you're right."

After she left, Michael settled back in his chair and stared into the fire as he finished his wine. All day his thoughts had kept drifting to Jess. She captivated him. The women he usually went out with were at least as interested in his money as they were in him. What they didn't understand was that it wasn't *his* money—at least not most of it. It was his family's money. His grandfather and then his father had devoted their lives and careers to creating Morgan Estate Winery. Building on that was as much an obligation as it was his legacy. He loved the business, and he especially loved the challenge of turning it into a diverse enterprise.

He wasn't sure how Jess would react when she found out who he was, but he had a hunch she wouldn't be any more impressed than if he really was on the hotel's catering staff. Dinner with her was going to be interesting, as was discovering what it would take to convince her to sell the bar. He knew it wouldn't be easy, but he never backed away from a challenge.

LATE SATURDAY MORNING Jess unlocked the front door of the Whiskey Sour and punched in the code to deactivate the alarm. It was no longer being monitored—that was one of the bills she hadn't been able to keep up with—but she and Eric, the part-time bartender, were the only people who knew. She tossed her department-store bag onto the bar and switched on the lights, then went into the kitchen and turned on the deep fryer so it would heat up by the time she opened.

Trying on clothes was one of her least favorite ways to spend a Saturday morning, but the shopping expedition had been less painful than expected. She and Paige both loved a good bargain, and her friend had flair without being flamboyant. Now Paige was stopping to buy coffee and muffins and bring them to the bar while Jess got ready to open for the day. She quickly put away the glassware she'd left in the dishwasher the night before, checked the keg room to make sure the lines were clear and primed, and inspected the two restrooms to make sure there were no surprises. Thankfully, there weren't.

Paige came in juggling an umbrella and a paper bag. She set the bag on the bar and opened her umbrella. "I hope you don't mind if I set this over here to dry. It's really coming down out there."

"No problem." Jess locked the door and went back to the bar to inspect the contents of the paper bag. "What'd you bring?" Her stomach was rumbling and she couldn't wait to find out what her friend had brought to eat.

"Two nonfat lattes and a couple of chocolate chip muffins." Paige immediately looked guilty. "I should be watching my weight, but those muffins are too yummy to pass up."

Jess took the two paper cups out of the bag and snapped the lid off one of them. "You do *not* need to watch your weight. You're only a size twelve, and besides, Andy obviously likes you just the way you are."

A delicate flush colored Paige's flawless skin. "I'm not so sure about that…and I'm actually a size fourteen."

"Fourteen, shmourteen. You are gorgeous and Andy is crazy about you." She took a sip of coffee. "Mmm. I needed this. How much do I owe you?"

"My treat. You can get them next time."

"Thanks." She appreciated Paige's generosity, especially since she'd just unloaded a sizable chunk of this month's grocery money at Macy's. She couldn't remember the last time she'd given this much thought to what she was going to wear, or spent money that could have been put to better use. Her guilt was compounded by memories of her mother shopping for slinky clothes to wear when she went to the bar trolling for men. *Damn it, this is* not *the same thing. You are* not *your mother,* she told herself.

Oblivious to Jess's momentary uncertainty, Paige took the muffins out of the bag. "Oh, good. They're still warm."

Grateful for the distraction, Jess headed for the kitchen. "I'll grab a couple of plates."

Paige settled onto a stool and Jess took the one at the end of the bar when she returned. For the next half hour, she decided, she would enjoy her friend's company and not think about money, guilt and her mother. "Have you heard from Rory?" she asked.

"No." Paige took a bite of her muffin and rolled her eyes in ecstasy. "Mmm, this is *so* good. What about you? Have you heard from her?"

Jess broke her muffin in half and inhaled the scent of warm chocolate. "No, but I didn't really expect to." She licked the chocolate off her fingers. "She loves Disneyland, and I'll bet she's having a great time giving her new family the grand tour."

Paige took off her glasses and cleaned them on the lower edge of her oversize burgundy sweater. "Speaking of families, Maria called yesterday. She took the baby for a checkup on Monday and she weighs twenty-one pounds already."

Jess assumed that was a good thing. "It's kind of amazing to think that of the five of us, Rory and Maria are now parents."

"I wouldn't have minded if it had happened sooner," Paige said. Jess knew she had been dreaming about motherhood since they were in college.

"If it had, you'd be a single parent right now." This

was one of Jess's least favorite subjects, but she couldn't let it drop. "No offense, but I grew up with one.…"

Paige reached for her arm and gave it an affectionate squeeze. "I know, hon. You had it rough, but lots of single parents do a great job. Look at Mitch and his daughter before they met Rory. Single parenthood was thrust on him when his wife died, and he's a great dad."

Jess immediately regretted her thoughtless comment. "You're right. Not everyone ends up with a mother like mine. That's something to be thankful for."

"In spite of that, you're one of the most grounded, sensible people I've ever met. And I know it's just as well I'm not a single parent, but I can't help hoping that someday…"

"It'll happen. If anyone's going to end up a childless old maid, it'll be me." They both laughed, but Jess knew her friends secretly agreed there was a lot of truth in that. "You, on the other hand, are moving on with Andy."

Paige looked troubled. "I'm pretty sure Andy doesn't want to 'move on' with me."

"What happened? Did the two of you have a falling-out over something?" Jess sipped her latte and gave her friend a sly grin. "You seemed to be getting along *very* well at Rory's wedding."

Paige didn't blush. Her face went radioactive.

"Oh, my God. You and Andy…did the two of you…?" Paige turned even redder, and Jess couldn't resist finishing the question. "Do the deed?"

Paige kept her eyes lowered, as if she'd committed some kind of crime, and she swirled a stir stick through the froth on her latte.

"You did!" What was it about weddings? Rory had hooked up with Mitch at Nicola's wedding. Paige and Andy got together at Rory's, and Michael had probably been thinking along the same lines when he asked her to dance. It was a typical guy thing, which meant it was probably what he hoped would happen after their dinner meeting. He could think again.

"We did," Paige said. "But we shouldn't have. We *wouldn't* have, except I think we both had too much to drink that night."

Jess finished her coffee as she took this in. *Looks like you're the only the one who went home alone that night,* she thought. *Typical.* "You and Andy are adorable together, not to mention perfect for each other. And for the record, I saw you and Andy leave the reception. I'm a bartender, remember? I see my share of tipsy people, and neither of you were intoxicated. At least, not on alcohol."

Paige gave her head a rueful shake. "The next morning was awful."

"How so?"

"It was awkward, and I mean *painfully* awkward. There we were…naked in my bed…and we're just friends, for heaven's sake! Neither of us knew what to say, and all I could think about was how much I didn't want him to see me without clothes on."

A normal person would have been amused by Paige's discomfort over waking up with a gorgeous guy like Andy in her bed, but a sick feeling coiled in the pit of Jess's stomach. The need to keep her body covered and private had become second nature. How many times had one of her mother's creepy boyfriends brushed against her inappropriately or barged into the bathroom while she was in the shower or—she shuddered—while she was using the toilet? Sometimes that had been accidental, but there had been other times when she'd absolutely known it wasn't.

Nothing like that had happened to Paige, but she was unnecessarily self-conscious about her weight. Jess pushed aside her own insecurities and focused on her friend. "You need to stop worrying about this. You're beautiful, with or without clothes, and Andy obviously thinks so, too. Have you talked to him about this?"

Paige looked chagrined. "No. We get together for burgers and beer every Wednesday after work, but I canceled this week."

Jess was the last person to be handing out relationship advice, but she couldn't let this go. "You're adults, you're both single, you're good friends. Seriously, there shouldn't be any regrets."

Paige sighed. "I know, and I will talk to him. I just wish it hadn't happened. Now, can we talk about something else? Like your date with Michael."

"It's not a date," Jess reminded her. "It's a business dinner."

Paige pointed to Jess's shopping bag. "Oh, yes. Business. And that required new clothes because…?"

Because her wardrobe was far from businesslike. She'd had decent clothes when she was a high school teacher, but since taking over the bar she had gradually sold most of them at a consignment store in an attempt to keep up with the bills. Now she had a closet filled with old shirts, faded jeans, a couple of pairs of sneakers, a collection of completely impractical bridesmaid dresses and the equally unwearable shoes that went with them.

"Have you found out anything about him?" Paige asked.

"He's commissioned some paintings from Rory's mom. Nicola's husband is his lawyer. And he seems to know a lot about wine."

Paige leaned on her elbows, hands under her chin. "He must have money. I like him better already. What's his last name?"

"I don't know."

"What kind of business does he want to discuss?"

"He's going to open a wine bar here in SoMa and he thinks he can talk me into selling the Whiskey Sour. To him."

Paige sat up and examined the sleeve of her sweater, suddenly intent on a loose thread. "Would that be such a terrible idea?"

"Um…*yes!* I'd be letting Granddad down if I sold it. Besides, I love this place and…okay…I know it's not a home, but in some ways it's the closest I've ever had." And she had always loved working here.

"I know, sweetie, but it's been such a struggle for you to make ends meet."

True, but she wasn't throwing in the towel. "It's been a tough slog, but I'm more than just a bartender. I'm a businesswoman, and I really have learned a lot about the hospitality industry." She didn't mention the possibility of getting a bank loan so she could fix up the place. Given Jess's less than stellar track record for managing money, Paige probably wouldn't approve of that, either. She was all about stability and playing it safe.

"How long can you keep going like this?"

Jess shrugged. "As long as it takes."

Paige put an arm around her shoulder. "I guess as long as you're happy, that's the most important thing."

Jess glanced up at the clock. "Speaking of business, it looks like I'm open."

"And I need to use the restroom," Paige said. "Then I'd better get going. I'm still not finished packing."

Jess unlocked the front door and flipped the switch to turn on the red neon open sign. She was clearing away their cups and plates when Paige burst out of the women's washroom, struggling with the zipper on her jeans.

"Oh, my God! All I did was flush the toilet, I swear, and now it's overflowing and flooding the bathroom and I can't make it stop!"

Damn it. This was the third time this week. She rushed into the storage room, grabbed the plunger and a mop, and wheeled the bucket into the women's restroom.

Stupid damn plumbing. What have I done to deserve this?

Chapter Five

Jess used a few choice words on the toilet as she rammed the plunger into it several times. That seemed to do the trick, for now at least.

Paige hovered in the doorway. "I'm sorry. Do you need some help?"

"Everything's under control." She was becoming adept at this.

"I'm *so* sorry."

"It's not your fault. There must be a blocked pipe or something." One of her patrons might've flushed something down there, and she shuddered to think what that might be.

"Are you going to call a plumber?"

On the weekend? That would cost a small fortune. "I'll call someone on Monday," she lied. She was at least grateful to the plumbing gods that it was the women's restroom and not the men's that had the problem. Relatively few women frequented the Whiskey Sour, and she had started using the men's room when no one was around. When Larry and Bill came in after work on Monday, she'd ask if they knew anything about plumbing. No point asking Eric, because he was even less familiar with this than she was.

After she mopped up the mess, she dumped the contents of the bucket down the men's toilet and was rolling it back to the storage room when the door opened. A customer already and it was only noon. This was promising.

Paige was cleaning her eyeglasses again, but quickly put them back on to see who had come in. She looked as surprised as Jess felt. It was not one of her regulars. Not a handful of locals who thought they'd try something different. Not some misguided tourist. This was young woman about their age, and she was alone. Maybe not a customer after all. Was she lost and needing directions? Change for the parking meter?

She was taller than average—even taller than most men—with short, sleek dark hair. She was wearing jeans and a jacket, casual clothes, to be sure, but there was no question they had designer labels stitched into them. And she looked vaguely familiar, although Jess couldn't place her. "Can I help you?" she asked.

The woman walked up to the bar, oozing confidence, and took a stool. "Sure. I'll have a beer." She glanced at her watch. "And I'll take a look at the menu, too."

"Oh. Sure." Jess shrugged and exchanged a quick glance with Paige. "I'll be right with you."

Paige gave Jess a hug and went to retrieve her umbrella. "I have to go. Have a good week, and be sure to call me after your date. I'll be dying to hear how it went." From the door, she reiterated her request by holding her hand to the side of her head, her thumb and pinkie extended in the universal call-me hand sign.

I give up, she thought. Why was it so hard for everyone to accept that this wasn't a date? She waved goodbye to Paige and handed a menu to the woman at the bar. "I'll be right back," she said.

She stopped by the women's restroom and slapped an out-of-order sign on one of the stall doors. Back behind the bar, she washed her hands and turned her attention to her unexpected customer. "What kind of beer can I get you?"

"Do you have an English-style bitter?"

"Sure do." Jess wouldn't have pegged her as someone who knew anything about beer, let alone had a taste for it.

"Great. I'll have one of those." She scanned the menu again. "The grilled vegetable panini sounds delicious."

Jess reached for a glass. "Sure thing." She'd bought the panini grill, figured out how to use it and printed new menus, hoping that might bring in some new business. There were two problems. Her regulars didn't want paninis. Guys like Larry and Bill weren't into "fancy food"—they wanted plain old peel-and-stick grilled cheese sandwiches. And she couldn't afford to advertise, so the rest of the world didn't know that the Whiskey Sour now served kick-ass paninis.

Jess filled the beer glass and set it on a coaster. In what had become the bar's sorry excuse for a kitchen, she prepared the veggie panini and placed it in the press to grill. She went back into the bar to find the woman looking around with interest.

"This is kind of a cool place. How long have you worked here?" she asked.

Jess knew she was just making conversation, but it seemed like a strange question. "A couple of years," she said.

"I see. It's not the kind of place I'd expect to have a female bartender."

True. That surprised a lot of people. "I'm not just the bartender. I'm also the owner."

The woman smiled at her. "Interesting."

She didn't say why she thought it was interesting, and Jess didn't know how to ask.

"Clever name…the Whiskey Sour. I like it."

"That was my grandfather's idea. He originally intended it to be a cocktail lounge, but he never quite got that to fly. Back when he first opened, the people who worked around here started coming in. They liked the place, mostly because everyone liked Granddad, but they wanted pretzels and beer, not appies and martinis."

"Does anyone ever come in and order a whiskey sour?"

Jess laughed. "Once in a while, but most of my customers are beer drinkers." *Like you.* The timer buzzed and she went into the kitchen to get the sandwich, still pondering the incongruity of this young, expensively dressed professional woman sitting in her bar. Alone, in the middle of the day, drinking beer.

"Here you go." She set the plate in front of the mystery woman and gave her a set of napkin-rolled cutlery.

"Thanks. This looks great."

"Thanks." Now, if the universe would just serve up another hundred or so customers just like this one, she'd be set.

"This is really good," she said after swallowing her first bite and another mouthful of beer. "So, do you own the whole building, or just the bar?"

"Oh. Um…the whole building." Complete with a

whopping big tax assessment and an ever-lengthening list of things that needed to be fixed.

"What's on the second floor?"

This was getting weirder by the minute. Not only was this woman not your typical barfly, she was asking a lot of questions. Like maybe she was from the tax department, trying to figure out how to squeeze even more blood out of this particular stone.

"There's an apartment and some office space, but they're empty right now." Her granddad had lived up there for years, but when she'd come to stay with him as a teenager, he had moved them into a bigger place and found a tenant to take the apartment. The last renters had trashed the place and the last business to lease the office space had run into some legal problems and shut down last year. Now the apartment wasn't fit for human habitation and the office space seriously needed to be modernized. Without the rental income she couldn't afford to fix either of them, and until she did she couldn't find reliable tenants.

"I heard your friend say you were going on a date. New man in your life?"

"Um…not a date. It's just a business dinner."

The woman smiled. "Mixing business with pleasure can be fun."

Getting dating advice from a friend was one thing, but from some random person who had just happened into the bar was just plain weird. Maybe it was time to ask a few questions of her own. "What brings you to SoMa?"

The visitor looked completely nonplussed. "Business," she said. "I just wrapped up a meeting and thought I'd grab a bite to eat."

A Saturday business meeting? That ruled out the possibility of her being a tax assessor. She hoped. "Are you in real estate?"

"In a way. Not sales, though. More on the design end of things." That sounded kind of vague, but maybe she really had just wandered in for lunch and was simply asking questions instead of talking about the weather.

"I plan to fix up the bar one of these days," Jess said, more for the sake of conversation than anything else.

"What do you have in mind?" The woman looked around with renewed interest.

"Oh. Well, I'm not really sure. I mean, I've always thought a fifties theme would be fun. Kind of in keeping with the name and what my grandfather had in mind when he opened the place."

"You're right. That really would suit the name. You could install a bank of crescent-shaped booths along that side wall, an old jukebox, put in a dropped ceiling with a stardust theme…" She paused. "Sorry. I tend to get carried away with stuff like this."

"No, those are great ideas. Just not in the budget, I'm afraid." If the bank loan came through, she would still have to do a lot of the work herself. With the exception of the damn plumbing. If it didn't, she might have to give up her apartment and move into the dump upstairs in order to pay for a plumber.

"It's fun to daydream. Do you have color scheme in mind?"

"Turquoise."

The customer looked impressed. "Good choice. Turquoise and cream vinyl upholstery, lots of chrome accents. Very retro but with a modern edge. I like it," she said, as if the ideas had all been Jess's.

Jess leaned her elbows on the bar and looked around, seeing the place through new eyes. The woman was right. Booths would be perfect and so would the stardust ceiling. Eric would love it.

"Now I just need to convince the bank to lend me the money." It was a long shot, but what the heck.

"And a building permit," the woman said. "Then you're all set."

"Really? I'd need a building permit for that?"

"You need a permit for everything."

No kidding. Taxes, licenses, permits. Some days it felt as if everyone wanted a piece of her pie.

The door opened and a boisterous group of college-age men came in, laughing and talking. They shoved two tables together and settled themselves into chairs.

"Excuse me a minute," Jess said to the woman at the bar. She was pretty sure some of these young guys had been in before, but she checked everyone's ID anyway. "What I can get you?"

"Two pitchers of Bud," one of them said.

"Better make that three."

The others nodded their agreement.

Great.

"How about some nachos?" one of them asked.

"Yeah, good idea. Do you have nachos?"

"You bet," Jess said. "One order?"

"Better make it two to start with."

"You've got it." She liked the sound of "to start with," even though it meant she could end up with a group of drunk college boys on her hands. She could handle them, but they'd still be a pain in the butt.

Behind the bar she set a pitcher under the tap, and while it filled she put half a dozen glasses on a tray.

After she topped up the pitcher and moved it onto the tray, she filled another. The woman sitting at the end of the bar was watching her and it made her a little uncomfortable, although she wasn't sure why. She set the second pitcher next to the first, hoisted the tray off the counter and carried it to the already raucous group.

"Two nachos and another pitcher coming right up," she said after she served the beer.

Their animated discussion about a sporting event rendered them oblivious.

By the time she served their food, two of the three pitchers had already been consumed. "Would you like another?" she asked as she picked up the empties.

"Yeah."

"Keep 'em coming."

It was going to be a long afternoon.

"Can I get you anything else?" she asked the woman at the bar.

"No, thanks. How much do I owe you?"

Jess rang in the beer and panini and handed the check to her.

She took out a slim leather wallet that matched her handbag and extracted a couple of bills. "Here you go. Keep the change." She glanced at the table of college boys as she tucked her wallet away. "Do you always work alone?"

"Oh. No, not all the time. My part-time bartender will be in this afternoon."

"That's good. I imagine some customers can be a bit of a challenge."

"They can, but I've never had a problem." Learning how to handle jerks had been the one good thing that had come from her hellish childhood. Being here on her own bothered her from time to time, but the bar was rarely busy during the daytime, even on a Saturday. Most drunks were easy to handle—they just needed to be humored, and the difficult ones were no match for a sober person with kick-ass self-defense skills.

"Well, it was nice to meet you. Great sandwich, by the way. And good luck with your renovation plans. I hope that works out for you."

"Sure, thanks."

Instead of leaving, though, she went into the women's restroom.

Damn it. All Jess could do now was keep her fingers crossed that the one functioning toilet didn't malfunction.

One of the rowdy, beer-swilling young men waved an arm at her. "Hey, barkeep. Can we get another couple of jugs over here?" That was followed by a round of laughter and applause.

She sighed and reached for a pitcher. At moments like this even she questioned the wisdom of trying to keep this business afloat. She scanned the room and pictured a crowd of elegantly dressed professionals seated on turquoise vinyl and sipping martinis. First thing Monday she would call the bank and see if she could light a fire under somebody.

MICHAEL PACED ACROSS the living room of his Nob Hill apartment, phone in hand, waiting for Lexi's call. This kind of downtime was rare, and it wasn't by choice.

His email in-box was empty. Ginny had sent the final proofs of the labels for the new wine, and he had approved them. She had also sent a draft of the winery's

next newsletter. He had read and made some suggestions on that.

Drew Attwell had forwarded a status update on the
purchase of new bottling equipment for the winery.
Michael had replied with a question and a couple of
comments.

He had called the manager of the wine bar at the
wharf to reserve a table for dinner with Jess on Thursday
evening, and then he'd started laying the groundwork
for his plan to persuade her to sell her business. He'd
spoken to his real estate agent and arranged to pick up
the keys for the Folsom Street building. It was a long
shot, but showing it to Jess might garner some empathy.
Then he would take her to Morgan's at the Wharf, and
she was sure to be impressed. Who wouldn't?

Thinking ahead to that evening was making him
impatient. What was taking Lexi so long? This project
was in limbo until he found out what she thought of
his plan to acquire the Whiskey Sour and to find out if
she'd come up with a strategy for making an offer that
the present owner couldn't refuse.

He checked his watch. One o'clock and still no call.
He was sure she would have wrapped this up by now.
Lexi was a stickler for detail, but even so he couldn't
imagine what the holdup might be.

He sat down and opened his laptop to check his
email. Nothing. He snapped it shut again and strode
across the living room to the bay window. The rain that
had been falling since early that morning had grayed
out the view from his top-floor apartment. He might
have bought a place in the city long ago if this classic
old Nob Hill apartment hadn't met his needs and been
so comfortable. Vanessa had been all for helping him

find the perfect place, but he had stalled, knowing that shopping for real estate together would have her thinking it was *their* perfect place instead of just his.

His mood was starting to match the weather. Patience wasn't one of his virtues. His father had often cautioned him about rushing ahead to get things done. *Good things come to those who wait.*

Good things also came to those who made them happen.

He was debating whether or not to call his sister when his phone rang. It was about time.

"Lexi?"

"Hi, Michael. How's it go—"

"This took longer than expected. Is there a problem?" He regretted the words the moment they spilled out.

"Jeez. You're welcome. Don't mention it."

"I'm sorry. That was out of line." He forced himself to stop pacing. "I appreciate everything you're doing. I hope you know that."

"Of course I do. And this might have taken longer than you expected, but I had planned to spend all morning at the building on Folsom Street. And it was good to be there on such a wet day because I saw firsthand just how bad the roof is."

He didn't like the sound of that. "Did you have time to drop by the Whiskey Sour?"

"I did." She didn't continue.

"And…?" She knew he was anxious to hear what she thought, and that gave her the chance to push his buttons by making him wait. She'd been doing this since they were kids, and his reaction was her payoff every time. "You met Jess? What did you think?"

"I thought you wanted my assessment of the building."

"I do."

"Then why are you asking what I think of her?"

"I'm not."

Lexi laughed. "Yes, you are. And for the record, I really like her. I'll also tell you that you've got a good shot at buying the building *or* at landing the girl, but there's no way you'll get both."

Where was this coming from? "What makes you think I want both?"

Lexi laughed. "I understand why you wanted me to look at the other locations—none of them have ever been a bar or a restaurant and they'll need a lot of work and money to turn them into one—but you didn't need me to look at her building to know it's a much better prospect. The Whiskey Sour is already a bar, so all the bones are there. Sure, it needs work, but a lot of it is cosmetic."

Okay, he liked the sound of that. As for the owner…

"Seriously, Lex. What makes you think I want both?" This was business. Sure, Jess was attractive—beautiful, really—and dating her would be a nice change from the Vanessas of the world, but he wanted the bar. Besides, Jess wasn't his type.

Who are you kidding? His "type" was a gold-digging social climber, and he was tired of them. Jess was no more interested in social status than she was in him. Oddly enough, that made her more attractive. Damned hot, actually.

"What makes me think you want both?" Lexi asked. "Hmm, let's see. She's gorgeous. She has something you want. You've never been known to back away from a challenge. All the signs are there, bro, but you have to make a decision."

His mother doled out dating advice all the time, but Lexi? This was new. And as fascinated as he was with Jess, she was not his top priority. "I want the building," he said. And he meant it.

"All right. If that's what you want, I'll help you get it. If you change your mind and decide you'd rather have the bartender, you should buy the building on Folsom Street."

Jess must have made quite an impression on her. "What are your thoughts on how I should approach this when I see her on Thursday?"

"She doesn't have a clue about running a business. Only one toilet in the women's washroom is working, and that's against code. Her business license has expired, or if it's been renewed, the new one hasn't been posted. And she's talking about borrowing money to renovate the place but didn't know she needs a building permit if she's going to move ahead with that. I have a meeting at city hall on Monday, so I'll poke around and ask a few discreet questions while I'm there."

City hall. Interesting. He hadn't thought of that angle, but with Lexi's connections, they might be able to nix Jess's chance of getting a permit, or at least keep her tied up in red tape long enough that she'd have no choice but to sell. He brushed aside a twinge of guilt and reminded himself he'd be doing her a favor. She would walk away from this deal with a sizable chunk of change, and he'd have the perfect place for Morgan's South of Market.

"How long were you there?" he asked. "Did you have a chance to look around?"

"Long enough to have a beer and a sandwich."

"Was the place busy?"

"No. A friend of hers was leaving when I arrived, then it was just me until a group of frat boys came in."

Interesting. It hadn't seemed like a college hangout.

"She was having some kind of plumbing disaster, and then the college boys were being…well…boys. It takes a gutsy woman to work alone in a bar."

A sense of something approaching apprehension tightened his chest. She'd been working alone the day he'd dropped in, but he hadn't considered the ramifications. Those two old-timers—Larry and Bill—were as protective of Jess as her grandfather would have been. She seemed confident and secure in her surroundings, but working alone in a place like that, in that neighborhood, could definitely be dangerous. Even for a woman who was trained in self-defense.

"Did you get the impression there could be a problem?" Maybe he should drive over there on some pretext or other.

"I got the impression that anybody who gives her any trouble is going to get his ass kicked. And she did mention that another bartender would be there tonight."

"That's good," he said, trying to imagine what her reaction would be if he dared go in and check up on her. Somebody's ass would get kicked, all right.

"I have to get back to my office, Michael. Do you still want my report on the Folsom Street building or are you going after the Whiskey Sour instead?"

Lexi made his business strategies sound cold and impersonal when that couldn't be further from the truth. Jess was struggling to keep her business afloat. Selling it to him would solve her problem and his. "Yes, I should have the report on hand, just in case—"

"In case you get the girl instead?"

He laughed lightly. "You and Mom have more in common than you'd like to believe."

"Ha-ha. I need to add a few more specs and finish up a couple of sketches, then I'll email my report to you early in the week."

"Thanks, Lexi."

He set his phone on the coffee table next to his laptop and paced across the living room a couple of times, processing everything his sister had said. Especially the part about getting the building or getting Jess, but not both. He knew what he wanted, and when he made up his mind to do something, failure was not an option.

Spending time with Jess was just an added bonus. She was smart, she made him laugh, she didn't seem at all interested in his money and she was an eyeful. That didn't mean he *wanted* her, not in the sense Lexi meant, but since meeting her last Saturday night, he had thought a lot about being with her. Any man would have been attracted to her in that strapless gown. She had been ridiculously awkward about how much creamy-white skin was on display and intent on not showing any cleavage.

The next time he'd seen her, the smooth skin and subtle curves had been hidden beneath boy's clothing, and her confidence and lack of guile were downright sexy. Would he like to be the one to teach her that she was a beautiful sexy woman who had a body that deserved to be celebrated? Hell, yes. As arrogant as that sounded, even inside his own head, he had the experience to know what she needed, and that he could give it to her. Even thinking about it was a turn-on and he was a man of action, which meant that hanging around here at loose ends was a dangerous thing. Dropping in on her right now was the last thing he should do, and the thing he wanted to do most.

Best to put a little distance between them. He grabbed his phone and speed dialed the house in Napa Valley.

"Mom?" he said when she answered. "It's Michael. I have some work to catch up on this weekend and I thought I'd do it at home. I hope that's okay with you."

"Of course. Is everything okay?"

"Couldn't be better. Too many distractions, though." At least that part was true. "I'll work better at home."

"Will you be here for dinner?" Her voice sounded hopeful. "We'll eat around six if that's okay with you. Ben will be thrilled."

"Dinner will be great. I'll be there in a couple of hours." Before his impatience got the best of him.

Chapter Six

On Thursday evening Jess dashed into the Whiskey Sour half an hour before Michael was due to arrive. When she'd started getting ready, this had just been dinner. A business meeting. The longer she fussed, the more it felt like a date. She had started with a soak in the tub, but refrained from shaving her legs. Date or no date, his legs were not going to encounter hers.

Three times she'd applied and removed eye shadow, and each time it was either too dark or too lopsided or just plain too trashy. She finally gave up and settled for mascara. Her hair was a similar story. Leaving it down always seemed to attract too much attention. She tried leaving some down and sweeping the top and sides back, but the clip kept sliding sideways. In the end she had brushed it all into her usual ponytail and fastened it with an elastic. After that she'd spent far too much time ironing a crease into a pair of slacks, and then she'd broken down and shaved her legs anyway, all the while telling herself she was wasting her time because *this was not a date*.

The bar was actually busy, for a change. Okay, not *busy*, but busier than usual. Two couples shared a table by the front windows. Three young men were huddled around a pitcher of beer at another table. Larry and Bill occupied their usual stools at the corner of the bar, even though it was well past their usual departure time. No need to ask why they were still hanging around. She plunked her backpack on the bar and shrugged out of her windbreaker. After she pulled off her helmet, she shook out her ponytail.

Eric was behind the bar, filling small white bowls with salted peanuts. He stopped midpour and looked her up and down. "I thought you had a date tonight."

"It's not a date. I'm going out for dinner."

"And that's what you're wearing?"

"She looks pretty good to me," Bill said.

Larry nodded his agreement.

"Thank you," she said to her two best customers, making a face at Eric. "I went shopping with Paige and she helped me pick out this sweater set."

Eric set the jar of peanuts on the counter and gave her his you've-got-to-be-kidding-me look. "You expect me to believe *this*—" he made a sweeping head-to-toe gesture in Jess's direction "—*this* was Paige's first choice for a dinner date?"

"Not her *first* choice." Paige's first choice had been a sleeveless red cocktail dress that required panty hose and shoes that were not sneakers. More specifically the shoes she'd had to endure at Rory's wedding, but no way was she was wearing those torture devices again.

Paige's next choice had been a too-short skirt that revealed too much leg. Her third had been a slinky emerald-green satin camisole that put too much emphasis on her lack of cleavage. Paige said it actually turned that deficiency into an asset, but Jess wasn't buying it. Not the compliment, such as it was, and definitely not the skimpy, overpriced camisole. She had settled on a soft apple-green sweater set she could wear with the slim-fitting black pants she'd bought two years ago to wear to her grandfather's funeral. The sweaters had been expensive enough, even though they were on sale. And they were practical. Sort of.

The bank was still giving her the runaround over the loan, and as of this afternoon she had just enough money in her account to pay her liquor suppliers, Eric's wages and next month's rent on her apartment. If tonight's patrons hung around and ordered a couple more rounds of drinks, she might even scrape together enough to pay the phone bill.

"There's nothing wrong with what I'm wearing. Paige says it's a good color for me, and she let me borrow a purse—" She hauled the black-and-green tapestry handbag out of her backpack and opened it. "And these." She pulled out two necklaces. "One casual and one dressy. Once I find out where we're going, I'm supposed to tell him I need a few minutes to get ready, go into my office and put on the appropriate jewelry."

Eric held one necklace in each hand. "I'll grant Paige this. The girl has good taste and she definitely knows how to take something from blah—" another head-to-toe hand wave "—to…less blah."

Jess rolled her eyes. "What's the point in getting all dolled up for this guy? For one thing, it's not my style. For another, I'm pretty sure he's after something and once he realizes he isn't going to get it, he won't ask me out again."

"You think this guy expects you to put out on your first date?"

"No! And if he does, he'll *really* be disappointed."

There was no point in reminding him this wasn't a date. No one believed her anyway.

"So what does he want?" Eric slid a bowl of peanuts in front of the two men at the bar.

"The Whiskey Sour."

"No way," Larry said.

Bill shoveled a small handful of nuts into his mouth and shook his head.

Eric's smile faded. "What do you mean?"

"He's looking for real estate in this area to open a wine bar, and *my* bar is exactly what he wants."

"Where'd he get the idea it was for sale?"

"Since it's not for sale, I have no idea. He seems like the kind of guy who assumes he can have anything he wants."

Eric leaned against the back counter, looking thoughtful. "A wine bar, huh? What did you say his name is?"

"Michael."

"Michael…?"

"I don't know."

"Oh, sweetie. You're going out with this guy and you don't even know his name?"

"It's not like he's a total stranger. He knows Rory's mom."

"And he's a big tipper," Larry said.

"And a car buff," Bill added. "He's restoring an old Morgan."

"Is he, now? It's about time our girl landed herself a man who has money *and* class." Eric tweaked her ponytail. "Did Paige have any advice about what to do with your hair?"

"No," she lied, fluffing up her bangs and smoothing out the rest. "What's wrong with it?"

"You look like the girl next door."

"What's wrong with that?"

"Well, let's see. You're not sixteen and this is not high school. You're going out for dinner." He winked at the two men sitting at the bar. "A *business* dinner that could possibly turn into a date."

"I'm sure it won't be anything fancy."

"Still, it's hard to believe Paige didn't suggest something for your hair."

Jess quashed the momentary flicker of guilt over her misrepresentation of her friend's fashion sense, but not before the eagle-eyed Eric detected it.

"I know that look." He grabbed the purse and opened it.

"Hey! Where are your manners?"

"Aha." With the flourish of a magician he pulled a green-and-black polka-dot scarf out of the purse as if it was a big white rabbit. "I knew she'd think of something."

"Give that back."

"Turn around," he told her. "We can use the scarf as a headband."

Larry nodded his agreement. "Good idea," Bill said. "Lose the ponytail. Men go for women with long hair."

It was one thing to accept fashion advice from Paige, who was a total clotheshorse compared to Jess, and from Eric, for whom the same could be said, but an old bachelor mechanic? That's where she drew the line. "The ponytail stays. Paige said I can tie this around it." She reached for the scarf.

Eric whisked it out of reach. "Okay, fine. You can keep the ponytail, but I'll do the tying. Turn around."

Jess reluctantly did as she was told.

"I almost forgot," Eric said while he worked on her hair. "Some guy from the health department showed up today."

Oh, crap. Now what? "Did he say what he wanted?"

"Yeah, he was here to check out the plumbing. Says you need to get the plumbing in the women's restroom fixed, ASAP. And your business license has expired."

Double crap. This was no coincidence. Somebody must've called the city and complained. "Did he leave his name?"

"He left his card. I put it on the desk in the office."

Jess wondered how much time she could buy. "I'll call him in the morning and—"

The door swung open just as Eric finished with the scarf. Michael stepped into the bar, instantly seemed to size up the situation and flashed her a smile.

The sick feeling brought on by her worries about having to pay for a plumber was replaced by an unexpected increase in her heart rate and rapid rotations of her stomach. This was crazy. She had already seen him in a perfectly tailored suit at the wedding, and in what had clearly been expensive business attire the day he dropped in to the Whiskey Sour. Tonight, dressed in a pair of casual, dark-colored cords, a button-down shirt and black-and-gray argyle sweater, he should look less sexy. He didn't.

Eric's hands settled on her shoulders. "*This* is your date?" he whispered in her ear.

Jess nodded, at a surprising loss for words.

"Too bad."

"Why do you say that?" she asked over her shoulder.

"Because it means I can't ask him out," he teased.

She applied an elbow to his rib cage. "Behave."

Eric had other ideas. "So you're Michael," he said, extending one hand across the bar.

Michael confidently walked up to the bar and accepted the handshake. "I am."

"I'm Eric. Jess's relief bartender and sometimes fashion consultant."

Michael switched his attention to Jess. "Nice work. You look beautiful."

"Thanks." Should she say something about how he looked? While she pondered that, he took a stool and shook hands with Larry and Bill.

"So where are you two crazy kids off to tonight?" Eric asked.

"I thought I'd take her to Morgan's at the Wharf."

"Sounds like a nice *casual* place for a first date," Eric said, glancing pointedly at Jess's things that were still strewn across the bar. "Can I get you something?" he asked.

"No, thanks." Michael smiled at Jess again. "Whenever you're ready…"

"Right. I just need a couple of minutes." She scooped her things off the bar. "Be right back." She hauled everything into her tiny office and left the door ajar so she could hear their conversation.

"You wouldn't happen to be Michael Morgan, would you?" Eric asked.

"I am." And he didn't sound surprised.

She sure as heck was. How did Eric know who he was?

"Jess said you want to open another wine bar in this neighborhood."

"Crap."

She typed San Francisco after his name.

"Bingo."

Michael Morgan, CEO of Morgan Estate Winery.

Michael Morgan, owner of Morgan's on Nob Hill. A wine bar.

Michael Morgan, owner of Morgan's at the Wharf. Another wine bar.

Michael Morgan, benefactor, California Down Syndrome Society. Okay, that was probably a different Michael Morgan.

From what she could see, the Michael Morgan who was sitting at her bar—eating peanuts and having a friendly chat with Eric, Larry and Bill—was loaded. At least now she knew why he required the services of a corporate lawyer and knew so much about wine. She smacked her forehead. No wonder he'd looked so surprised when she said wine tasting was pompous. And now there was no question about his motive for being here. He wanted the Whiskey Sour. "Think again, Mr. I've-Got-More-Money-Than-I-Know-What-To-Do-With Big Shot. It isn't for sale. It wasn't for sale last week, it isn't for sale now, and no amount of wining and dining is going to change that."

"Jess?" The door swung open and Eric stepped into the office. "Are you ready?"

She hastily closed the search engine. "Yes. All set." She stood and grabbed her windbreaker and the borrowed handbag.

"Aren't you forgetting something?"

"What?"

"The reason you came in here, remember?"

She did not.

"The necklace?"

Right. She picked up the string of black and silver beads and slipped it over her head, but it got snagged on her ponytail and the scarf.

Eric disentangled them and settled the necklace in place, then rolled his eyes when she stuck an arm in the sleeve of her windbreaker. "You couldn't have worn a nicer jacket?"

"I rode my Vespa, and this is the only thing I have that's wind and waterproof."

"It's not raining."

"But it might."

"You're hopeless," he said, shaking his head. "So... what did you find out?"

"What do you mean?"

"Don't give me that innocent routine. You looked him up on the internet."

"I found out why he's interested in this place."

Eric gave her an affectionate hug. "Is it so hard to believe that maybe he just wants to take you out for dinner?"

"Yes. Nobody gets that rich without pushing other people around."

"And everybody knows that nobody pushes Jessica Bennett around." Then Eric flashed her a smile. "No one's going to force you into anything you don't want to do, so I think you should just relax and have a good time. Besides, they don't come any dishier."

"You're hopeless." He was also right. Michael Morgan was the dishiest.

MICHAEL OPENED THE CAR DOOR for Jess and closed it after she slid in. Since she had emerged from her office she had yet to make eye contact, and he didn't know why. Aside from Heather Franklin, the girl he'd persuaded to go to junior prom with him, Jess was the most reluctant date he'd ever had.

He slid behind the wheel and fastened his seat belt. "Is that your scooter?" he asked, referring to the pint-size, candy-apple-red motorcycle parked in front of him.

That got her attention. "It's a Vespa, and yes, it's mine. How did you know that?"

The tone of her question implied that he had somehow been spying on her. Did that mean she was onto him, or just suspicious by nature? "After I got here you carried a helmet into your office."

"Oh."

Time to change the subject. "I need to make a quick stop before we go for dinner," he said. "I hope that's okay."

"That's fine with me."

All right, then. Time to put his plan into action. Neither spoke as they drove the short distance to the building on Folsom Street. Along the way he glanced at her a couple of times to see if she was looking at him. She wasn't.

The abandoned building looked even less welcoming than he remembered. "This is the place I'm considering for the new bar. My architect asked me to check on a few things." That was the truth, although not entirely accurate. Lexi had sent her report as promised and they had done a walk-through two days ago. Bringing Jess here was simply a strategy for opening a dialogue about the work and the costs involved in renovating one of these old warehouses.

He got out of the car and went around to open her door. "Come on in and have a look."

While he unlocked the door, she craned her neck and looked at the building's shadowy facade. After the door swung open, he groped for the light switch. He switched it and nothing happened. He switched it off and back on again, and a couple of overhead fluorescent tubes reluctantly flickered on.

Oh, God. This place better not be rat infested. Technically this was not a first date, but it wasn't the time for a woman to see how squeamish he was about vermin.

Jess followed him inside, and her stunned silence spoke volumes.

"It doesn't make a good first impression," he said.

"No offence, but this place is a dump." She walked into the middle of the dilapidated warehouse and looked around. "It's a lot bigger than it looks from the outside. What kind of seating capacity do you have in mind?"

Not large enough to fill this space. "I'm going for a casual, intimate setting, so no more than fifty or so. My…ah, the architect suggested dividing the space with interior walls to make several smaller rooms for private wine tastings, meetings, that sort of things."

"Oh. Good idea."

Did she really think so, or was she just humoring him? He made a pretense of inspecting the central pillars and an electrical panel on one of the side walls while she walked toward the back of the large space, carefully picking her way around a stack of wooden pallets and scattered debris on the floor. Apparently, she didn't share his rat phobia.

Her ponytail swung from side to side as she moved. He'd been hoping she'd wear her hair loose, like the night of her friend's wedding, but no such luck. He smiled as he recalled walking into the bar and seeing her employee, Eric, tying it up with the scarf. Now the big question was, would she let Michael undo it?

No, not tonight, because he wasn't going to try. Sleeping with her would be the surest way to blow a potential business deal.

She stopped, turned around and walked back.

"What do you think? Does this seem doable?" he asked when she rejoined him.

The question seemed to puzzle her. "I guess so. I'm not good at visualizing this sort of thing, though. What are you going to do with the second floor?"

"It's been used as office space in the past, so we'll probably lease it after it's been renovated. Should be a good way to generate some revenue."

"Also a good idea."

"Your building has a second floor. What do you use it for?" Lex had already told him, but he was hoping Jess might elaborate.

"There's an apartment and an office."

"Occupied?"

She sighed. "I wish. The last tenants stiffed me for two months' rent, then trashed the place and moved out. Some kind of consulting business had been renting the office, but last year the police showed up and arrested the owners and I haven't seen them since."

"Ouch. That kind of bad luck gets expensive."

"Tell me about it." He waited for her to elaborate, but she didn't.

He considered asking a few more questions but decided to back off. "I think I have all the information I need. Are you ready to go for dinner?"

"Sure."

He held the door open for her and locked up while she waited by his car.

"I gather you're the owner of Morgan's at the Wharf?" she asked after they were under way.

"I am. Have you been there?"

Her ponytail swung back and forth when she shook her head.

"Then you're in for a treat. We have a limited menu—mostly seafood—but an extensive wine list."

"Both red and white, I assume?" Her eyes sparkled the way they had when she'd described the Whiskey Sour's wine list the night they met.

He liked that she had a sense of humor, and a somewhat self-effacing one at that.

"Plenty of both. I think you'll be impressed." Most women were when they found out he was the CEO of Morgan Estate Winery. Jess didn't seem to be, but he was confident that by the end of the evening, he would have a better idea of what made her tick.

"I have to confess…I have an ulterior motive for taking you to my place."

She swiveled sideways. "Your place? We're going to *your* place?"

Without taking his eyes off the road, he could feel her suspicious gaze boring into the side of his head. "Morgan's," he said. "At the Wharf." What did she think he meant? His…oh, God…his *apartment?* Seriously? *What kind of lowlife does something like that?*

Instead of responding to his explanation or asking what his ulterior motive might be, Jess folded her arms around herself, tightly, and turned away.

Hell, he shouldn't have brought it up at all. It would

be better to have that conversation over dinner, and so much easier to get a read on her reaction when they were sitting face-to-face. What was it about this woman that interfered with his usual good judgment? Until he figured that out, he'd better watch his step.

"That's the plan."

She stole a surreptitious look at her dinner date. Everything about Michael Morgan was flawless. His clothes, his smile, his height. He even had the perfect haircut, especially compared to present company.

Larry made up for thinning hair and a receding hairline by letting the sides grow too long and covering the top with a ball cap. Bill had very little hair at all. Eric's chin-length sandy-blond waves were unabashedly girlish. Jess kept her own carefree long hair tied back off her face, and she trimmed her own bangs to eliminate the expense of going to a salon. Michael had the kind of precision haircut that required constant maintenance and a steady cash flow.

She edged away from the door. *Who is this guy, and what do you really know about him?*

His name was Michael Morgan, and he was taking her to Morgan's at the Wharf. A person didn't have to be a genius to add that up. He wore expensive clothes, drove an expensive car and he was opening a wine bar.

Another wine bar.

She hung her backpack on a hook and stashed her helmet on a shelf next to a stack of printer paper. Then she shoved aside a pile of bills and set the borrowed purse on the desk next to the computer keyboard. The purse strap jostled the mouse, and the monitor flickered to life. Jess snuck another peek past the door. Michael was munching on peanuts and laughing at something Larry was saying.

She sat gingerly on the edge of the ancient desk chair so it wouldn't creak and opened a search engine.

She got more than 29 million results for Michael Morgan.

Chapter Seven

You are such an idiot, Jess scolded herself. When was she going to learn not to overreact to every little thing? *Michael is* not *a man who has to trick a woman into going to "his place." Seriously, look at him!*

She'd been so certain that tonight was about him coercing her into selling the Whiskey Sour, but then he'd taken her to that dump on Folsom Street, and he seemed intent on buying it. He'd hired an architect and everything. Now that she knew who he was, she could safely say he was savvy enough to believe she had no business expertise worth sharing. Maybe Paige was right. Maybe he really did want to go out with her and this really was a date.

Relax. His motives would be revealed soon enough. If he was still after the Whiskey Sour, he could think again. If he thought the evening was going to end with the two of them back at "his place," well, he could think again.

Fisherman's Wharf was one of the busiest parts of the city, even now that the summer tourist season was over, and the red neon sign at the entrance to a parking lot said it was full. Michael merely waved at the attendant as he drove in, then pulled into a spot marked Reserved. Must be nice.

As they crossed the parking lot, his hand lightly touched her back, just long enough to guide her toward the glassed-in pedestrian overpass that led from the garage to Pier 39, then he dropped it. They hadn't spoken since she'd misunderstood his reference to "my place," and she had a feeling that the silence bothered her a lot more than it did him.

"How long have you been in the wine bar business?" she asked.

His response sounded easy and relaxed, as though they'd been having a friendly chat instead of being stranded in uncomfortable silence. "We opened here two years ago. The place really took off, so we looked for a second location in Nob Hill."

And now he was looking at SoMa, so she assumed the second bar was doing as well as this one.

At the entrance he opened one of the plate-glass doors and held it for her. "Here we are."

They were greeted by a dark-haired woman in an elegant but understated knee-length black dress that had a high neck and long sleeves. Jess saw that as a positive sign. She hated places where female staff were expected to wear skimpy, revealing clothing.

"Michael, it's wonderful to see you."

"Good to see you, Kathryn. I'd like you to meet a friend of mine, Jess Bennett."

She extended her hand and gave Jess a warm smile. "Welcome to Morgan's at the Wharf. Is this your first visit?"

Jess accepted her handshake—impressed that it was firm and confident—and smiled back. "Yes, it is."

"Then you're in for a treat." She shifted her gaze to Michael. "Your table's ready."

She didn't say "your usual table," but it was clear that it was. Every table was optimally situated to take advantage of the view and maximize intimacy, but his— theirs—was even more private.

How often does he bring his dates here? She let out a little sigh. *Does it matter? You're not one of them.*

"Thanks, Kathryn." Michael held Jess's chair for her, and she settled into it while she took in the view of Alcatraz. The bay sparkled under the setting sun and the gulls swooped and soared over ferries and other boats moving around the harbor.

Inside, the decor hinted at a nautical theme without being obvious. Much more "bon voyage" than "ahoy, matey." Ha. The designer hadn't missed the boat on this one. The dark polished wood and shiny brass accents were tempered with modern overhead lighting positioned to create an intimate circle of light at each table. The strips of wall between the large windows were adorned with colorful watercolors of windswept beach scenes that Jess immediately recognized as the work of Rory's mother, Copper Pennington. One of her paintings was pricey. This collection had to be worth a small fortune.

The table setting was casual chic. Cream-colored linen tablecloth and matching napkins, gleaming cutlery, a narrow glass vase with a single white calla lily, and two large wine goblets that glittered with reflected light.

The financial investment must've been huge, and the payoff was obvious. Morgan's at the Wharf offered a quiet, classy retreat from the teeming energy of the city's most popular tourist destination, and now that she and Michael were seated, every table was occupied. As her granddad used to say, this is how the rich get richer.

"Have you decided on a wine?" Kathryn asked.

"A bottle of pinot gris," Michael said. "The 2005, if we still have it."

"Right away." She smiled graciously as she slipped away.

"I hope you like seafood," he said.

"I do." She'd caught glimpses of shrimp cocktails and great bowlfuls of steamed mussels on other tables, and her mouth was already watering. Kathryn hadn't given them menus, though, and she suspected that Michael planned to order for them. Under almost any other circumstance that would annoy her—not that it had ever happened under any circumstance—but he was being charming, she liked that he had such a good rapport with his employees, and she felt oddly comfortable with going along with whatever he had planned for them. Within reason.

"Good. Seafood is our specialty."

Kathryn returned with the wine and held the bottle so Michael could inspect the label. After he nodded, she set it on the table and unfolded a waiter's corkscrew. "I think you're going to enjoy this wine," she said to Jess. "It's one of Michael's favorites."

She removed the foil, quickly twisted the corkscrew into the cork and removed it with that a soft, gentle pop that pleased the ear of even a non–wine drinker. She poured a small amount into Michael's glass and stepped back.

He went through all the steps he'd shown her at the wedding—the swirl, the look, the smell, the taste—all of which seemed unnecessary, since he already knew he was going to like it. He set the glass on the table. "It's perfect."

Kathryn poured some into Jess's glass, then Michael's. "Do you know what you'd like to order?" she asked.

"We'll have the seafood platter and a Caprese salad."

"Excellent." And then she was gone. Several waiters were serving patrons at the other tables. Kathryn's only table was theirs.

"No one does shellfish better than our chef." He picked up his glass and held it out to her.

She lifted hers, touched it to his, then it gave it a gentle swirl. "It has legs," she said.

He grinned at her. "You've been doing your homework."

"Google comes in handy for all kinds of things." Wine-tasting terminology. Winery owners.

He studied her thoughtfully. "I'm sure it does."

She knew he was waiting for her to taste the wine. She made a pretense of smelling it first. "Fruity."

He was leaning back in his chair now, apparently still amused.

She didn't dare try to guess which fruit—she would almost certainly be wrong—so she took a sip and made a point of letting it wash over her tongue before she swallowed. It was good. Very good, actually. "I like it. It has a subtle citrus flavor. Nice crisp finish."

"You're a quick study."

Damn right she was. "Is this from your winery in the Napa Valley?"

Finally, a question that caught him off guard. "You really *have* been doing your homework."

"Google," she said again. "I didn't know your last name till tonight. I did a quick search before we left the Whiskey Sour."

"Did you, now?" His eyes, thick lashed and dark blue in this light, shone with amusement. "Yes, this is one of ours. What else did Google tell you?"

"That you own a winery in the Napa Valley and two wine bars here in the city."

"That's all?"

"There's more?"

"I have no idea. I've never looked for myself on the internet."

She suspected she had barely scratched the surface of Michael Morgan's web-worthy achievements. "Neither have I. I'm not interesting enough for there to be anything about me online."

"I find that hard to believe."

Oh, please. She didn't want to talk about herself, which meant it was time to change the subject. And she might as well get to the point of why they were here. "You said you had an ulterior motive for bringing me here. Are you going to tell me what that is?"

He took a long slow sip of his wine, then he set the glass down and leaned a little closer. "Are you always this direct?"

"Almost always."

"I see. Well, I meant what I said about wanting you to see the wine bar here at the wharf, and I'm also interested in your thoughts on opening one in your neighborhood. We're going for a unique atmosphere, wine list and menu at each place, but we still want each to maintain the signature Morgan experience."

She wanted to believe him, but her more suspicious side was having doubts. He had to be after something. "You've seen the Whiskey Sour, twice, and you still think I'm qualified to offer advice on how to run a wine bar?"

He laughed lightly. "Don't sell yourself short. You run a bar in SoMa, so I thought you'd be able to tell me what type of clientele to expect, what kind of atmosphere they're after, that sort of thing."

Should she believe him? If this was an indication of what he had in mind for his new enterprise, he could anticipate a very different clientele from hers. "The Whiskey Sour has been there for years. When Grand-dad opened it, he catered to people who worked in that neighborhood—especially mechanics and guys who worked in the autobody shops. To some extent we still do." Unfortunately, there weren't so many blue collars these days. "That's starting to change now that condos and loft buildings are bringing in new residents and other businesses are opening in the area."

Kathryn appeared with a basket of warm French bread, set white ceramic plates shaped like scallop shells in front of each of them and disappeared again.

"I knew it would be a good idea to run this by you," he said. "You're brilliant."

"Oh, well, thanks," she said, feeling more baffled than brilliant.

"A classic-car theme could be perfect, something from the fifties. Without being clichéd, of course. Lots of chrome and glass, aluminum garage doors that can be rolled up to open up the space or rolled down to separate the private tasting rooms that my—" He paused. "That the architect suggested."

"Sounds amazing," she said. *Glad I could help.* She wondered if, along with the corporate lawyer and the architect, he also had a plumber on retainer.

"Ah, here we go," he said.

Kathryn was back with a huge platter, liberally loaded with clams, mussels and scallops, and oysters on the half shell. The steam rising from this feast was lightly scented with garlic and herbs. She set an empty bowl next to the shellfish, and then the salad. "And here's your Caprese."

Jess had never seen such an unusual salad. It consisted of slices of tomato and soft white cheese arranged on a plate, drizzled with olive oil and balsamic vinegar and garnished with fresh basil leaves. It looked delicious.

Kathryn poured a little more wine into their glasses. "*Bon appétit*," she said as she left them to enjoy their feast.

Jess's taste buds had died and gone to heaven. She helped herself to a generous sampling of seafood, careful to avoid the oysters. Which were the first things Michael took, she noticed. He picked up one of the shells and handed it to her. "Try one. You won't find a better oyster anywhere in the city."

Much as she loved seafood, in her opinion there was no such thing as a good oyster. "Are they cooked?" They didn't look cooked. They looked as slimy as if they'd just been shucked.

He set one on her plate, picked up one from his and slid the revolting blob into his mouth. He chewed it slowly, swallowed and chased it with a sip of wine. "You don't know what you're missing."

"Sorry. I've never liked oysters."

"Try one."

She didn't want to seem ungracious, so she picked up the shell, let the offensive mollusk slither onto her tongue and closed her eyes, fully expecting her system to reject it.

She opened her eyes and chewed. *Who knew an oyster could be* this *good?*

"What did I tell you? We only serve the best."

"I'm impressed." She kind of hated to say it, but it was true. "I wish I could do something like this with the Whiskey Sour."

"What's stopping you?" He seemed genuinely interested in what she had to say. "You told me you have plans to renovate. What do you have in mind?"

She'd been thinking about fixing the plumbing, installing a new dishwasher, maybe a couple of bar stools, and doing a little advertising to see if that would attract some new customers. Providing she could convince the bank to lend her the money, of course. That was before the mystery woman had come in for lunch last Saturday and started her dreaming about a retro cocktail lounge. Now she was rethinking everything. Or she would be as soon as she got the stupid health inspector off her back and figured out how she'd scrape together the money to pay for a building permit.

The vintage-car theme wasn't as appealing as her fifties-themed cocktail lounge with crescent-shaped booths upholstered with turquoise vinyl, but she could frame her granddad's photos of the cars he had restored over the years. Her friend Rory was really into vintage stuff—she'd have tons of ideas.

Right. You're not even sure you can pay this month's

phone bill. She didn't need a bank loan. She needed a miracle. No way could she afford to close the bar and get by with no income while she spent money that wasn't hers on renos she couldn't afford. Still, she wasn't sure she should tell him exactly what she had in mind, in case he thought that was brilliant, too.

"Business was dropping off even before my granddad got sick. By the time he died, his savings were pretty well gone." When she'd taken over, it hadn't taken long to burn through her own meager funds. "I'd like to re-decorate the bar so it's more in keeping with the name, but that'll depend on whether or not the bank will lend me the money."

"You own the building, don't you? That counts for something."

"Not as much as you might think. They still expect me to put up some of my own money." He didn't need to know she had none, although he'd likely guessed that was the case. He also didn't need to know that she was struggling to pay off a student loan for a college degree that got her a job she hated, and that she had a credit rating that was…spotty. Much as she hated to admit any similarity between her and her mother, she grudgingly acknowledged that she had inherited her mother's less-than-stellar ability to manage money.

Michael studied her thoughtfully over the rim of his wineglass. "You could always sell it."

She should have been angry, and she damn well would have been if he hadn't been so predictable. At least the real reason for this charade was finally out in the open. "Like I told you, it's not for sale. If that's what this is all about…" She gestured at the spread on the table. "You've wasted your time, and your wine."

He looked unfazed. "Not a waste at all. I'm looking for a building and you're having financial problems. If you change your mind, this could be the best solution for both of us."

Okay, *now* she was mad. How did he dare presume to know what was best for her? "Not everything is about the money, and the Whiskey Sour is *not* just a building. It's my home. I love that place. I'll figure out a way to make it work." Her earliest memories were of visiting her granddad at the bar. He used to give her little jobs to do—stacking coasters, rolling cutlery in napkins and, as she got older, counting the float before he put it into the till. When she was a teenager and went to live with him for good, it had become her home. Not even Mr. Tall Dark and Filthy Rich had enough money to buy that out from under her.

No doubt he thought the Whiskey Sour had more potential than the rat hole he'd shown her earlier. Anyone could see that. If he didn't want the building on Folsom Street, he could keep looking.

"Relax. It was just a suggestion."

He poured a little more wine into her glass, but not his own.

"Aren't you having any more?" she asked.

"Not if you want me to drive you home." He picked up the salad plate. "More for you?"

She shook her head. So that was it? He was just going to change the subject and pretend this conversation never happened?

He helped himself to the last few slices of tomatoes and cheese. "So you gave up a career as a teacher to take over your grandfather's bar."

It wasn't a question, so she didn't respond.

"It was *that* important to you?"

"It was. Granddad practically raised me, since I was a teenager anyway, and he was the only family I had." The only family who mattered.

"Did you live with him?"

"Yes, since I was fourteen."

He looked interested, but not surprised by that. "Where are your parents? Are they…?"

"Dead? No, my mother lives in Stockton." Should she tell him about her father? For all she knew, he was dead. Maybe that *would* shock him. "I've never met my father."

Michael looked at her, unblinking. He took his time to respond and when he did, it wasn't the response she expected. "If he wasn't going to stick around, then maybe that was for the best."

She set her fork on her plate. Apparently, nothing took this man by surprise.

"I'm sorry," he said. "That sounded insensitive, and what I meant was—"

"Hey, don't apologize. My granddad used to say the same thing. My mother's a lousy judge of character." And Roxanne Bennett's self-esteem was so low, it couldn't get any lower. When it came to men, those two characteristics were a disastrous combination.

"If your father wasn't around, what made you decide to leave? Did you and your mother not get along?"

"We were okay when she was between boyfriends, but when she had a man in her life, it was like I was invisible." It was true, or at least it was the only way Jess could rationalize having a mother who risked her little girl's safety for a romp in the sack with a string of men she didn't know.

Michael's jaw tightened with disapproval.

Finally, a chink in that carefully constructed armor? "One of them cornered me once when my mom wasn't there." She folded her hands in her lap and stared down at them. "It didn't end well."

She'd been fourteen, and she'd come home from school one afternoon to find her mother's latest—a washed-up, unemployed drunk called Buzz—sprawled on the threadbare sofa, the TV remote in one hand, drinking beer straight from the can.

"Where's my mom?" she asked.

He didn't take his eyes off the TV. "Out."

That was helpful. Not. Jess slipped her backpack off her shoulders, pushed aside some dirty dishes on the kitchen table and set it down.

"Wanna beer?" Buzz asked, laughing.

Funny. "No, thanks."

He belched. "More for me." Judging by the number of flattened cans strewn on the floor and coffee table, he'd already had more than enough.

She debated whether to stay and clean up the kitchen, hide out in her room, or leave the apartment and come back later. If her mom wouldn't be home for a while, she didn't want to be stuck here with Buzz, but she didn't particularly want to hang out in the rain, either. She hated the mall, but at least it would be warm and dry. Safe.

Buzz heaved himself off the sofa and staggered into the kitchen. "Can you cook?" he asked.

"No." She started filling the sink with hot water and dirty dishes, her senses on full alert, and suddenly she was trapped between the counter and the disgusting mass of flab hanging over the top of Buzz's pants. One arm snaked around her waist—the one with the tattoo of the naked woman on it. He pawed at her breast with one meaty hand and grabbed her crotch, hard, with the other. The smell of alcohol and body odor filled her nostrils and fear fed the swell of nausea that rose in her throat.

Her survival instincts kicked in, big-time, crowding everything else out of her mind. This moron had a mean streak a mile long and easily outweighed her by 150 pounds, but this could *not* happen. She couldn't let it.

He pressed his erection against her rear end and fumbled with the zipper of her jeans, and she willed herself not to throw up. *Oh, God. Do something!* But trying to fight him off would not end well for her, she knew that.

When you're dealing with a drunk, you've got to keep your wits about you. That's what Granddad always said.

Use your head, she said to herself. *Make. Him. Stop.*

She turned off the taps, struggling to breathe, telling herself not to scream.

He yanked her jeans open and jammed a hand inside her panties.

No! *No way, you son of a bitch.* She fought off the panic, forced herself to stay calm, and did her damnedest to adopt one of her mother's sultry come-ons.

"Hey, big boy." Her chest was heaving, but she managed to keep her voice soft and low. "What's your hurry? If it's fun you want…"

It worked. With an evil laugh, he backed off enough to let her turn around and face him. "Like mother, like daughter." His sour breath assaulted her when he stuck his tongue in her mouth.

She held her breath and squeezed her eyes shut.

Up. Yours.

She stroked the inside of his calf with the sole of her sneaker and pressed herself against the bulge in his pants, revulsion crawling over every inch of her skin like an army of ants.

Either too drunk or too stupid to suspect anything, he widened his stance.

She lowered her foot to the floor, braced herself against the counter and drove her knee into his crotch.

Buzz staggered back, eyes bulging, and fell to the floor in a writhing fetal position.

She grabbed her bag off the table and ran out of the apartment, leaving the disgusting scum lying in a pool of his own vomit. She never went back.

"Jess?" Michael's voice jolted her back to the present.

Damn it. She'd let herself go to the one place she hated. She picked up her wineglass, but her hand was too shaky. She set it back on the table so she didn't spill it.

Michael immediately covered her hand with his. "Oh, Jess. Did he…?" But he stopped, as though he wasn't sure what the question should be.

"He kind of made an indecent proposal." Her friends said she still had serious trust issues stemming from that incident. They were probably right. Much as she wanted to believe she had moved past that devastating day, it had changed who she was and thinking about it still made her feel like last week's dirty laundry. "I said no."

Michael relaxed his grip on her hand, but didn't remove it. She was glad for that.

"Then I left and went to my granddad's, and I stayed with him till I went to college."

"I hope you called the police."

"Granddad did, but since the guy hadn't actually 'done anything' to me, it would have been my word against his and there was nothing they could do."

"The bastard." At least that's what it sounded like, but he said it so quietly she couldn't be sure.

"In some ways I'm lucky. If one of my mom's boyfriends had tried that when I was younger, I might not have known what to do, how to say no, and mean it. At fourteen, it was *hell no!*" She smiled.

He didn't. "I have two sisters. If anything like that had ever happened to one of them, I would have—" He didn't say any more, and he didn't have to. He probably would have reacted the same way her grandfather had.

"Your sisters are lucky to have had someone who'll stand up for them. But..." She was going to say that many girls never reported these things, especially not to family members, and thought better of it. "I was lucky, too. My granddad was there for me and I didn't have to go back." She picked up her glass and drank a little more wine, wishing the whole subject had never come up. "This is really very good. So is the food, and this place..." She set the glass down and glanced around the room. "It's classy, the food and wine are great, it has a fabulous view. Whatever you decide to do with the building on Folsom Street, it's bound to be popular."

"Thanks." He was looking thoughtful now, and she couldn't be sure what he was thinking. She just hoped he'd stopped feeling sorry for her and her rotten child-hood, and that he'd given up on the idea of turning *her* place into a wine bar, because that was never going to happen.

Chapter Eight

Michael pulled up in front of the Whiskey Sour and parked behind Jess's Vespa. It was a cute little thing. He hoped he'd get to see her ride it sometime. She was already reaching for the door handle when he touched her arm. She swung to face him, eyes wary. She only had agreed to this evening because it was a business dinner. Things had almost gone south after he'd mentioned she should consider selling the bar, but he had salvaged the evening by letting that drop and getting her to open up about herself.

His hand was still resting lightly on her arm. "I'm glad you agreed to have dinner with me tonight."

"Thanks for taking me to Morgan's at the Wharf. The food was great." She didn't say she was glad to have spent the evening with him, but she didn't move her arm away, either.

"You've given me some good ideas for the new place. I appreciate it."

"Glad I could help."

He would rather not talk, especially if meant prolonging a mundane conversation. He'd wanted to kiss her when he'd watched her struggle with the strapless bridesmaid dress, when he saw her in the T-shirt, blue jeans and high-tops in the bar last week, and tonight he just plain old wanted to kiss her. Lexi was right. He wanted it all. Jess's directness was challenging, her unpretentiousness was sexy, her real estate was exactly what he was in the market for.

He now understood Jess's self-consciousness and her preference for inconspicuous clothing. What he didn't understand was how a mother could endanger her daughter by bringing abusive men into their lives. Jess hadn't said much about what had happened to her, and she hadn't had to. He'd watched her momentarily slip back into the past, and for those few seconds he knew she had gone to a bad place. If he wanted her to trust him, he had to move slowly.

"We could do this again sometime."

Her wariness faded. "I hate to admit it, but we've already exhausted everything I know about running a business."

He took her cynical self-evaluation as an encouraging sign and, not being one to miss an opportunity, he lightly ran his hand up her arm to her shoulder. "We haven't exhausted everything I know."

"I didn't ask for your advice." She said it with the same tone she'd used when she declined his invitation to dance.

"Fine. Just dinner, then." He kept his hand moving until the nape of her neck was cradled in his palm, gently held her chin with the thumb and forefinger of his other hand and then he moved in.

Her initial reluctance was evident in the firmness of her mouth. Undeterred, he gently worked her lips with his until they went soft. His body had the exact opposite reaction.

She didn't push him away—another good sign—and after a little light prodding from his tongue, her lips parted slightly. He took his time, testing her willingness to let him explore further.

Her indecision was short-lived and when she joined in with a little tongue action of her own, his self-control faltered. In the space of a heartbeat his need accelerated from desperately wanting to kiss her to desperately wanting...her.

She brought her hands up to his chest but didn't apply any force, so he brought her closer, as close as two bucket seats and a stick shift would permit.

Don't rush her. It was good advice, and although the light touch of her fingertips on his neck made stopping almost impossible, he knew he had to. If he moved too fast, she'd bolt like a scared rabbit. Still, he took his time ending the kiss.

"Wait here," he whispered against the soft skin in front of her ear. "I'll get the door for you and walk you inside." Even in the dim light from the streetlamps, there was no mistaking the ragged rise and fall of her chest and her desire-darkened eyes. At this stage of a relationship, the best strategy was to leave them wanting more. Stopping now was the right thing to do. He brushed one last light kiss across her lips. This time he could live with doing the wrong thing, but there was no way Jess could.

JESS STOOD INSIDE THE DOOR of the bar and watched Michael get back into that racy little car of his and drive away. As he'd asked, she had waited until he opened the door for her—even though letting a man do things like that wasn't in her nature—and walked with him to the door of the bar. She's wondered if he would come in, but didn't want to ask, and he didn't suggest it.

Instead, he'd taken her hand and squeezed it. "I'll call you."

Oh, please. Guys said that all the time, even when they had no intention of ever calling again.

"I'll call," he'd repeated. He'd let go of her hand and tweaked her nose.

Now, as she watched him drive away, she knew he would. Michael Morgan seemed like the kind of man who didn't say things he didn't mean. She moved inside and let the door swing shut. Eric was watching her. "How was your date?" he asked.

Until five minutes ago, it hadn't been a date. They really had talked business most of the time and even when the conversation had strayed to personal stuff, like why she's left home at fourteen, he had seemed attentive only in a polite kind of way. And then that kiss. *Holy crap.* That had been a kiss to end a first date. Exactly the kind of kiss she'd imagined when he'd compared it to tasting wine for the first time.

"It was good," she said in reply to Eric's question. "The dinner, I mean."

Eric was grinning. "Sister, I know *exactly* what you mean."

Was it that obvious that she had just been kissed? She peeked at herself in the mirror at the back of the bar. Her hair looked fine and her clothes were still on straight. Michael hadn't even touched them and yet she felt as though she'd been ravished—in a good way, of course—and she hadn't been anywhere near ready for the kiss to end.

Eric slung an arm across her shoulders, the way he'd

been doing since they were kids. "You should have let him take you back to your place instead of dropping you off here. You could have invited him up for a nightcap."

"My Vespa's here, and all my other stuff." She waved toward the office. "And I figured I'd help you close up."

"Gee, thanks. I've been rushed off my feet, as you can see."

Two tables were still occupied by a handful of patrons. "Did it get busy at all?"

"Busier than usual."

"Any trouble with the plumbing?"

"Not tonight."

"So let's hear it. Did your hot date make you an offer you couldn't refuse?"

She knew what he meant, but her face still went warm. "You know, I was sure that's what he was going to do, but he took me to look at the place he's thinking about buying…" She paused and rolled her eyes. "Total disaster, but I guess anything's possible when you're loaded. Anyway, then he took me to his place at Fisherman's Wharf and we drank wine and ate seafood and talked."

Eric gave her a knowing smile. "I knew it."

"What?"

"It's not the bar he's after, darlin'. It's you."

She'd like to believe that, especially after that kiss, but she couldn't let that cloud her judgment. There was a good chance he was trying to soften her up—but there had been enough magic in his kiss for her to want to believe Eric might be right. She also had to consider the mysterious coincidence of the health inspector's visit.

Michael didn't seem petty enough to do something like that—besides, it wasn't the sort of thing that could force her to sell the Whiskey Sour—but someone had ratted her out. If Michael hadn't done it, who had? And why?

MICHAEL POURED HIMSELF a glass of wine, settled onto the sofa and turned on his laptop. It was late, but he had a few business matters to clear up and he'd sleep better knowing they'd been taken care of. He clicked on the report Lexi had sent earlier in the day and gave it another quick read. The Folsom Street building needed a lot of work, but his sister's sketches of the proposed floor plan had exceeded even his expectations.

He opened a new email and addressed it to her.

Lexi,
Great work, as always. Thanks for being so quick and thorough, but I'll hold off on putting in an offer for as long as possible. Haven't given up on the Whiskey Sour. I'll work on the owner if you'll continue looking into things at city hall. Appreciate your help.
Michael

If Jess was as cash-strapped as she claimed to be, it was no surprise that the bank wasn't forthcoming with a loan. In theory, the bank could accept the building as collateral. In practice, a financial institution wouldn't want to be stuck with a run-down old building if she defaulted on the loan. Not in this economy. Given her self-professed lack of business acumen, that scenario was entirely possible.

Now he needed to come up with a good reason to see her again, although he had a hunch that if he simply called and invited her to dinner, she wouldn't say no. He had hoped she'd be open to a good-night kiss, but he hadn't expected her to be such a willing participant.

Lexi's warning ran through his mind. *You've got a good shot at buying the building or at landing the girl, but there's no way you'll get both.* He wanted one thing—a location for his next business venture.

If you change your mind and decide you'd rather have the bartender, you should buy the building on Folsom Street.

That wasn't going to happen, although next time he saw Jess he would definitely work on getting her to let her hair down. Now he just had to make sure there was a next time.

THE BAR HAD BEEN QUIET for a Saturday afternoon, but Jess was still looking forward to having Eric start his shift at six o'clock. Her friends were coming for drinks that evening and she was eager to join them. Rory and Mitch were back from their honeymoon, Nicola was bringing Jonathan, Paige had smoothed things out with Andy, and Maria and her husband, Tony, were driving over from Sausalito.

Michael had called yesterday to thank her for all the advice she'd given him. She knew he wasn't basing business decisions on anything she said but she was curious to find out if he'd given up on buying the Whiskey Sour, so she mustered the courage to extend what she hoped sounded like a casual invitation to join her and her friends. Michael had said he'd love to.

Once again that created the quandary of what to

wear, and she'd had to give herself several stern lectures about the pitfalls of dressing to please a man. Still, she wanted to look good. Okay, she'd kind of like to knock his socks off, but that wasn't going to happen, so she'd settle for looking presentable. As soon as Eric arrived she would run home, have a quick shower and, with a little luck, piece together something decent to wear from her meager wardrobe.

Eric arrived a little before six. He looked pale, except for the dark circles under his eyes. Even his gorgeous curls, which were usually primped and bouncy, looked limp.

"What's wrong with you?" she asked. "You look like hell."

He pointed to his neck. "Laryngitis," he croaked.

"You're one to talk. What happened? Did you just get out of surgery?" He was looking at the front of her T-shirt.

"Ha, ha. I had a run-in with a ketchup bottle."

He rolled his eyes.

"You sound like you should be home in bed. Why didn't you call?"

"Didn't want to mess up your plans to hang with your friends."

This made a significant mess of her plans, but she sure didn't expect the poor guy to work when he was sick. "Go home. I'll manage."

"But—"

"I'll call your friend Aaron. If he can't come in, I'll manage on my own." Aside from her friends, it likely wouldn't be that busy anyway.

Thank you. He mouthed the words without actually saying them.

"Go. Feel better." Soon. She gave him a gentle push toward the door. "Call me tomorrow and let me know how you're doing."

She dug out Aaron's phone number, dialed and got his voice mail. She left a message, even though he probably wouldn't hear it till tomorrow morning.

"Damn it." Why hadn't she asked Eric to stay for half an hour so she could run home and change her clothes? She could freshen up here in the ladies' restroom, but it hadn't occurred to her to bring extra clothes with her.

What were you thinking?

Eight hours ago she had *not* been thinking about what she was going to wear tonight. Now she was stuck with faded old jeans, a T-shirt she had splurted ketchup on that afternoon, a plaid shirt and a pair of Converse sneakers that were still damp with toilet water because the toilet had overflowed…again. She would have to scrape up enough money to hire a plumber, and she had to do it soon, because the health inspector had said he'd be back in a week.

Her two remaining customers signaled that they were ready for their bill. After they left, she went into the office and dug her emergency bag of toiletries out of the bottom drawer of the desk. Deodorant, a bar of soap, half a box of tampons and a sample-size bottle of moisturizer that was so old, she couldn't remember where she got it, never mind when. All perfectly usable stuff—well, all except the moisturizer—in the average emergency. Spending the evening with Michael looking the way she did right now was a code-red crisis.

Desperate times, desperate measures, she thought. She picked up the phone and called Rory.

She explained the situation and her friend agreed to bring everything she needed.

"Unless I can dig up a pair of traveling pants, I'm pretty sure my jeans are all too big for you. How about a skirt? I'm sure—"

"No! No skirts. The jeans I'm wearing will be fine, but I need a clean shirt."

"That's easy."

"Nothing fancy," Jess said. "Nothing too flashy, either, and nothing revealing. I don't want him to get the wrong idea."

Rory laughed. "And the right idea would be...?"

"That I look nice without him thinking I'm trying to impress him." *Or that I'm trying to get him into bed.*

"Then I'll be sure to bring something unimpressive," she said, still laughing. "It'll be fun to see everyone. Mitch and I are looking forward to it, and we'll come a little earlier than planned so I can get you all dolled up."

Jess sighed.

"I'm kidding," Rory said. "I'll see you soon."

TRUE TO HER WORD, Rory and Mitch arrived half an hour before the others. Somewhat surprisingly, there were already four people at one table and two more sitting at the bar. Not busy by anyone's standards, but busier than usual for this early on a Saturday evening.

Rory looked totally gorgeous in a pair of black skinny jeans and a sleeveless raspberry-colored turtleneck and gold jewelry. Mitch looked as if he couldn't get enough of looking at her, and it was easy to see why. Rory showed him to the gang's usual corner table and shed her jacket while Jess poured him a beer and made sure her other customers were good, then she was hustled into her office by Rory.

"I found something that fits the bill," Rory said, pulling a powder-pink top out of her tote bag. "I bought it on sale and haven't even worn it yet, so it's all yours."

It was not at all what Jess had in mind. "What else did you bring?"

"Makeup."

"That's it? I never wear pink. It clashes with my hair."

Rory shook out the top and draped it against Jess's shoulders. "It does not. Pink is perfect with your complexion. Now, stop stalling and put it on."

Jess reluctantly shrugged out of her plaid shirt and stripped off the stained T-shirt.

Rory's eyebrows shot up.

Jess glanced down at her ancient white bra that had seen better days. She felt like a kid being warned to put on clean underwear in case she was in an accident. *Too bad,* she thought. It wasn't as if anyone else was going to see it. She quickly pulled on the top and looked down at herself.

It was a baby-doll style that flowed to her hips from an empire waist. She kind of liked that part, even though it was a bit on the girlie side. But the upper part was as snug as could be, and even though it had long sleeves and a high scooped neckline, there was nothing modest about the way it clung to her breasts.

"It's perfect," Rory said. "I knew it would be."

Jess glared at her. "Perfect for you. I never wear things like this."

Rory smiled triumphantly. "I don't own anything that looks like the things you usually wear. You said you didn't want anything revealing. This is completely modest and it's not going to give anyone the wrong impression."

"I don't know…"

Rory shrugged. "It's either this or your dirty T-shirt. What was that, anyway?"

"Ketchup."

Rory laughed. And she was right. Jess couldn't even consider wearing what she had just taken off. She looked at her slightly distorted reflection in the old mirror behind the door and saw that Rory was at least right about the color. It actually didn't look bad on her at all. She wished her assets—modest as they were—weren't out there for the world to see, but there was nothing she could do about that now. She hated being ogled, and yet some secret part of her couldn't wait to see what Michael's reaction would be. The night they'd met, he had been amused by her lack of confidence in her dress's ability to keep her covered up, but come to think of it, she hadn't once caught him staring at her breasts the way some guys did. She hated that.

"I'm not done," Rory said. "Sit down so I can fix your hair and makeup."

Knowing better than to argue, Jess complied. A few minutes later her cheeks had been dusted with blush and her eyelashes tinged with mascara. Rory insisted on combing out Jess's ponytail and instead swept her hair away from her face and fastened it at the back with a large silver clip.

"Okay, *now* I'm done. Let's have a look."

Jess stood and made an awkward spin so her friend could survey her handiwork.

"Very nice. Even Eric would approve, and I'm sure

Michael will be completely unimpressed." Rory laughed and gave her a hug.

"Thanks," Jess said. "Come on, I'll make you a cosmo and check on my customers."

One more table had filled up, and Maria and Tony had arrived. Jess took orders and by the time she served them, Paige had arrived with Andy. After he held her chair, he took the one beside it and draped an arm across the back of hers, his hand resting affectionately on her shoulders. Paige fidgeted with her glasses, the way she always did when she was flustered.

"I see you two worked things out," she whispered to Paige before she took their drink orders.

From behind the bar, she saw Nic and Jonathan come in and join the others in the corner. Jess waved to them, poured them each a glass of red wine and added those to the tray with Paige's and Andy's drinks. Before she finished serving those, two thirtysomething guys in sweatshirts and ball caps came in and sat at the bar. They each ordered a pint of ale without taking their eyes off Jess's breasts. She slapped a couple of coasters in front of them, pulled the pints and resisted the urge to tip the beer into their laps when she served them.

By the time Michael showed up, the bar was crazy busy—way busier than it had been in months. Aaron hadn't called back and she gave up on hearing from him. She had also given up on a chance to sit with her friends. Not that she would ever complain about being busy, but the timing was terrible. On the bright side, the extra cash would cover the hole in her bank account after she'd shelled out the money for a building permit earlier this week.

Michael nodded a greeting to her and took a chair

next to Jonathan. Out of the corner of one eye she watched the two men talk while she mixed drinks and filled glasses and pitchers with beer. After she served those, she stopped by her friends' table, acutely aware that they were all waiting to see how she and Michael would respond to each other.

She stood on the other side of the table and made a point of smiling at him. "Let me guess," she said. "A Guinness?"

"Sounds good."

She checked the status of everyone else's drinks and hustled back behind the bar. He watched her while she wiped the counter, loaded glassware into the dishwasher and filled glasses. She knew that because every time she glanced across the room, they made eye contact.

Ever since she'd invited him, she had imagined how this evening would go, starting with Eric behind the bar and her sitting at the corner table with everyone else. Michael would sit beside her. They would bump elbows a couple of times and then one of them would swivel the chair to one side and their knees would connect. Their hands would accidentally touch a few times, and then he would finally lean over and say something into her ear, something only she was meant to hear. It would make her smile, and then after that they would talk and laugh as if they were the only two people in the world. He would stay after the others left. The only part of the daydream that wasn't fiction was the way he would kiss her good-night. She already knew *exactly* how that would go.

Idiot. See what daydreaming gets you? Disappointed.

And what did dressing to attract a man get her? A

couple of ball caps with wandering eyes. She did her best to ignore their asinine conversation and suggestive remarks, all of which were loud and in bad taste. If they weren't careful, one or both of them could still end up wearing their beer.

She grabbed a tray to do the rounds, take orders and pick up empties just as Michael joined her behind the bar. He was carrying a couple of empty glasses, including his own, which he set on the counter.

"Looks like you could use some help."

"Thanks. Would you like another beer?"

"Not right now. How about I clear the tables while you take orders?"

"Oh. You don't have to—"

He reached for the tray and bumped her elbow with his. "I want to. Besides, it looks like this might be the only way we'll get to spend any time together."

This was not how she'd hoped the evening would unfold, but she could use the help and she'd rather spend time with him than watch him from across the room. "All right, then. You're hired."

By the time she came back with the orders, he had cleared the tables, put the clean glasses back on the shelf and was refilling the dishwasher. His jacket, she noticed, had been tossed on the back counter and his shirtsleeves were rolled up to just below his elbows.

"Looks like you've done this before," she said.

"I know my way around a bar. What else can I do to help?"

She rattled off a couple of beer orders and he filled the glasses while she scooped ice into the cocktail shaker and mixed another cosmopolitan for Rory. "Oh, and my friend Paige would like another glass of white wine."

change left by a customer. Even the losers who'd been sitting at the bar all evening finally got a clue, paid their tab and left.

After the rush died down a bit, she and Michael finally joined her friends for a few minutes before everyone left.

"We'll have to do this again soon," Nicola said. "Next time Eric will be here and the two of you will be able to sit with us."

Maria's husband helped her to her feet. "This has been so much fun," she said. "I love being a mom, but you have no idea how good it feels to spend a couple of hours in adult company."

That was followed by a discussion of everyone's plans for Thanksgiving, then everyone hugged everyone else as they made their way outside.

Michael walked back to the bar with Jess.

"Thank you so much," Jess said to him. "You were a lifesaver tonight. You don't have to stay, though." She felt she had to say it, even though she didn't mean it. "I can take it from here."

"I'd like to stay, if it's okay with you."

Oh, it was more than okay.

After the last customer left and she locked the door, she was glad he stayed. He finished clearing tables and wiped them down while she cashed out, then he rejoined her behind the bar.

"When your friends were talking about Thanksgiving, you didn't mention your plans."

"That's because I don't have any."

"Would you like to?"

His question was unexpected. "I'll probably be here."

"Would Eric cover for you if you had plans?"

He would if those plans were with Michael. "What do you have in mind?"

"I'll be spending the holiday with my family up in Napa Valley. Would you like to join us?"

"Oh." Spend the holiday with his family? She hadn't seen that coming. "I don't know. I wouldn't want to intrude on a family gathering."

"You wouldn't be intruding—you'd be a guest."

She desperately wanted to say yes. "I'll have to check with Eric, make sure he's feeling well enough to cover for me." Although for all the business they'd get that day, they could just as easily be closed.

"I'll call you on Monday to confirm."

She had a million questions, starting with why he wanted her to meet his family. Or did he just feel sorry for her because she didn't have plans for the holiday? *Don't go there,* she warned herself. If it was a pity invitation, she didn't want to know.

"Can you excuse me for a few seconds? I should take out the trash and check the restrooms before I leave."

He reached for the bag of trash before she picked it up. "Point me in the right direction," he said. "I'll look after this while you deal with the washrooms."

She told him where the garbage bins were. In the men's restroom she picked up several crumpled pieces of paper towel off the floor. No surprises in the women's, and she was beyond grateful that the one functioning toilet hadn't acted up. A few more nights like tonight and she might be able to afford a plumber.

Michael was back when she was finished with the restroom. For the first time that evening, his gaze traveled over her body. The pace was leisurely and his intent clear. Her skin heated up underneath her clothes. Then he moved in and put his arms around her. His body was solid and warm against hers. "It's been a long night. I've wanted to do this for hours."

His naturally deep voice now had an even huskier tone. He could have been reading the phone book out loud and there would still have been no mistaking his intent.

"Me, too." Might as well be honest. He was back to making direct eye contact, and she knew that he knew she was thinking the same thing he was thinking.

He reached up to the back of her head and undid the silver clip. It clattered onto the countertop when he let it go, and then he combed the fingers of both hands through her hair. She closed her eyes and felt her mind go completely empty, aware of nothing except how incredibly gentle and unhurried he was. When she opened them again, he smiled and then he kissed her.

His mouth was more urgent than his hands had been.

She wound her arms around his neck and pressed her body closer to his, just enough to let him know she wanted this to last longer than their first kiss the night he'd driven her here after dinner.

He seemed to get the message.

His tongue touched hers with a quick teasing invitation, then it retreated. She RSVP'd with a similar move, and the party was on. Within seconds they were both gasping, his hot breath mingling with hers.

His hand made its way under the loose fabric of her top and his fingers drew fiery trails across her skin till they reached the lower edge of her bra and the snug-fitting band of her top. For a split second Rory's look of horror at the appearance of her no-longer-white cotton bra flashed through Jess's mind.

Was she really ready to let Michael to see it?

He nudged her clothing up till his fingertips found what they were searching for.

He obviously had more important things on his mind than the state of her undergarments, and now so did she.

"Is this okay?" he asked. He must have sensed her hesitation.

"Yes," she whispered. It was heaven.

He was a lot taller than she was, and her exploration of his shoulders and chest and abs showed that he was in amazing shape, but his size and strength weren't threatening. Everything about this man was exactly the opposite of that. He was gentle; he asked if what he was doing was okay and he made it clear that if she wanted to stop, he would.

She didn't want to stop.

One of his hands cupped her butt and drew her against him, close and intimate. That should have brought her to her senses, but instead she lost them altogether. She angled her hips against his and pulled away, choking out a little gasp as she did. Arousal, unaccompanied by fear, was new. She didn't want this to stop. Couldn't have stopped if she'd tried.

He groaned. "We need to do something about this."

"About what?" She couldn't imagine doing anything but prolonging the exquisite tingles that zipped through her body every time they connected.

"This. Here. This isn't my style," he said. "The first time I make love to a woman, I like it to be in a bed."

In spite of what had almost happened, this wasn't her

style, either. Especially not on a countertop after closing time—or worse yet, on a filthy floor—like some kind of sleazy bar skank.

Her mother's style? Unfortunately, yes.

Hers? No way in hell, no matter how aroused she was.

"And after the first time?" she asked.

He smiled suggestively. "After that, pretty much anything goes."

The possibilities of being in bed with him made her shiver, but the reality of what she had almost done here freaked her out. He lowered his head and gave her long, lingering kiss, but he kept his hands to himself this time. "You could come home with me." It wasn't so much an invitation as a statement of fact.

She could. God knows she wanted to, but she didn't do things like this. She could not sleep with a man on the first date. Or the second. When she was a kid, how many mornings had she been introduced to a stranger named Dave or Jim or…Buzz. The thought made her skin crawl. Never a last name, because her mother hadn't bothered to find out what it was. The memories still made her stomach turn.

She shook her head and backed away. "I…no. I'm sorry. I can't. It's…it's too soon." Better to let him think she was a two-bit tease than know for sure she was an easy roll in the sack.

"Jess." He grabbed her hands before she moved out of his reach. "It's okay. There's no pressure. I'm a patient man and I'll wait till you're ready."

Right. She wanted to believe him, but other men had said much the same thing, right before they said they'd call. Only, they didn't. No matter what men said, they weren't interested in women who didn't put out.

He threaded his fingers between hers. "I'll call you next week—"

She must've done a lousy job of covering her disbelief, because he stopped talking and drew her back for another light kiss.

"When I say I'm going to call, I'll call. You agreed to come home with me for Thanksgiving, remember? We'll need to work out a time for me to pick you up."

"You still want me to go with you?"

"More than ever."

She wanted to believe him, more than anything.

Chapter Nine

Jess had never ridden in a Porsche before she met Michael, but she could get used it. She'd also never been invited to a real family Thanksgiving celebration. No, that wasn't right. This was just the first time she'd accepted an invitation.

Early that morning, Michael had picked her up at her apartment because she hadn't been able to think of a reason for being at the Whiskey Sour that early in the morning. Instead of letting him in when he buzzed, she had left him standing at the front door while she raced downstairs. She wasn't embarrassed about living in such a small, sparsely furnished apartment, but she wasn't ready to let him see it, either. If he was miffed, he didn't let on. Instead, he lifted her overnight bag off her shoulder and gave her a bone-melting kiss. If that kiss was any indication, it was going to be quite a weekend.

Neither of them spoke while he maneuvered through traffic and onto the bridge. The silence felt a little awkward, but once they were out of the city, she relaxed and let herself enjoy the scenery. It had been ages since she'd had a chance to get away, and in spite of her apprehen-

"Coming right up." He reached around her for a glass and his arm brushed across her shoulders.

She poured the contents of the shaker into a cocktail glass and added it to the tray at the same time he set Paige's wineglass on it. Their hands touched. It was accidental and it would be dumb to think he felt the same sizzle she did, but he didn't pull away, either. She hoisted the tray off the counter and he stepped back so she could get by.

Working with him was easy—it felt natural. *You'd think we'd been doing this forever instead of fifteen minutes.*

"Would you fellows like another beer?" he asked the two guys in ball caps at the bar. Maybe they'd be more civilized with another man around.

No such luck. During the evening she kept her cool and ignored the two jerks whose ogling became more obvious with every glass of beer they consumed. If Michael even noticed she had breasts, he didn't let on. In that regard he was a perfect gentleman, which was just her luck because of all the men there, she might not have minded being ogled by him. She quickly discovered that working with him was a lot more fun than just sitting with him would have been. For one thing, she didn't have to come up with witty conversation—which she was really lousy at—and it provided countless opportunities for them to bump into each other. The first few times their hands and elbows and shoulders connected, it was accidental. After a while they didn't bother trying to avoid touching and it gradually became intentional. He made a point of brushing her arm with his when he reached for a glass, so she reciprocated by letting her hand linger next to his as he passed her a handful of

sion about meeting Michael's family, she intended to make the most of these two days.

"It's beautiful up here," she said.

"It's my favorite place in the whole world," he said. "It's prettier in the summer when the vineyards are in leaf, but there's something special about every season."

"Have you always lived here?"

He smiled, but didn't take his eyes off the road. "Born and raised. Third generation, actually."

Wow. "It must be nice to have roots."

That earned her a quick glance. "It's something we have in common."

She almost snorted, suspected their family backgrounds were about as different as they could be.

"We're both running businesses that were started by our grandfathers," he added.

She hadn't thought of it that way, but he made a good point. She had a strong emotional attachment to her grandfather's business. Maybe a little too strong, according to her friends.

His hand lightly touched her arm. "Jess?"

She looked up at him. "Mmm-hmm?"

"Does talking about your grandfather upset you?"

"No, not at all. You just reminded me of something a friend said a couple of weeks ago."

He didn't ask what that was, but somewhat to her surprise, she wanted to talk about it. He hadn't said any more about buying the building on Folsom Street, most likely because he hadn't, and she had a niggling feeling that he still thought he had a chance at buying hers, and she needed him to understand that wasn't going to happen. "After my grandfather died and I inherited the bar, I had to make a choice. I could sell it and carry on with my life as it was, without Granddad, or I could quit teaching and keep his dream alive. At the time, it was a no-brainer."

"And now?"

"My feelings haven't changed." She loved being her own boss—she just wished running the place was as easy as it had looked when her grandfather was doing it.

"Grandfathers have a way of making you want to follow in their footsteps. I used to tag along with mine around the vineyards and the winery. It always amazed me that he knew exactly when the grapes were ready to be picked, when the wine was ready to be bottled."

"Is he still alive?"

"No. He died when I was in high school and my father took up the reins. Dad passed away eight years ago—heart attack—and that's when I took over."

"Do you know when the grapes need to be picked?" she asked.

He glanced at her again. "I'm sure I would have figured it out if I had to, but I hired an expert winemaker and I leave it to him to make that call."

Must be nice. She'd love to hire people to do the things she wasn't good at or didn't enjoy doing. Like fixing the stupid toilets.

"You and Eric seem to be good friends," he said. "How long has he worked for you?"

"I've known him since we were teenagers. His father used to be our cook, and Eric has worked there a lot longer than I have." And he knew way more about running a bar than she did. "I don't know how I would have managed without him."

After that they fell into a comfortable silence. He drove the way she imagined he did everything—quickly and with confidence. His hands were light and firm on the steering wheel, and she found herself studying them often. The last time she'd been with him, those hands had done some magical things. Thinking about it now made her warm all over. She tore her gaze away and looked out the window at the scenery flashing by. She could have driven like this forever, but after a couple of turns that took them onto secondary roads, he took his foot off the accelerator and clicked on the turn signal.

"Here we are." He swung off the road and through an open gate onto a long, hedge-lined driveway. That led them to a circular cobblestone parking area in front of a massive, two-story stucco building that could be either a really big house or a small hotel.

After he stopped the car, Jess sat up a little straighter, suddenly feeling a lot more nervous than expected. "This is your home?"

He slipped an arm around her shoulder. "Yes, it is. What do you think so far?"

"Um…wow. Very impressive." And intimidating.

"We're just a normal family." He pressed a switch to release the trunk. "Come on. I'll get our bags and then I'll introduce you to everyone."

As she was climbing out of the car the front door flew open and a young man ran outside.

"Mikey! Mikey!"

"Hi, Ben. Happy Thanksgiving."

Ben pointed at her. "Who's she?"

"This is my friend Jess." He took her hand and tugged her toward the stairs. "I'd like you to meet my brother, Ben."

"I have a dog," Ben said.

Jess laughed, and at that moment she relaxed. "That's great, Ben. What's your dog's name?"

"Poppy!" he shouted. "I'll show you." He rushed back inside, hollering the dog's name at the top of his lungs.

She was still laughing when she looked up at Michael. "So it's Mikey, is it?"

"Don't even think about it."

"Why didn't you tell me about your brother?"

He shrugged and put an arm around her shoulders. "I like to see how people react when they meet him."

"Did I pass the test?"

"With flying colors." Her reward was a light, tantalizing kiss. They were, after all, standing on the front steps of his family home and she couldn't very well expect him to get too carried away, as much as she'd like it if he did.

"Michael?"

Michael slowly lifted his head and grinned at the woman in the doorway. "Hi, Mom."

Jess's heart took a downward dip in her chest and she couldn't even guess how red her face must be.

"This is my friend Jess Bennett." He tightened his hold on her shoulders. "Jess, I'd like you to meet my mother, Sophia Morgan."

Sophia gave her a quick but thorough once-over, then she smiled broadly. "Welcome to our home, Jess. Happy Thanksgiving! Come in, come in. Are you hungry? Michael will take your bag upstairs while I get you something to eat. How was the drive? Not too much traffic, I hope."

"Thank you." She wasn't sure what else to say

because she had already lost track of half the woman's questions. She glanced back at Michael, who just nodded and smiled. Was he saying that he had known his mother would approve? Whether Sophia did or not, she had taken this unorthodox first meeting in stride, and all Jess could think was thank goodness for that.

Sophia led her through an impressively large foyer, down a hallway and into the kitchen, which was really more like one of those great rooms Jess had seen in magazines and on TV decorating shows. The furniture and artwork had been carefully selected and arranged, and it all looked expensive.

"I'm still working on a few things for dinner. Have a seat here at the counter and I'll get you something to eat." She was a small dynamo of a woman with silvering hair and the same sharp, blue-eyed gaze as Michael.

The counter was a breakfast bar flanked by four up-holstered stools that ran the length of a huge, granite-topped island. Jess took one of the stools and glanced at her watch. It wasn't quite nine, barely past breakfast, and Sophia had only "a few things" left to do for dinner?

"What would you like?" she asked. "Coffee? Tea? Orange juice?" She slid a cloth-covered basket across the smooth granite surface. "Help yourself to an orange scone. They're Michael's favorite."

"I'd love some coffee." She glanced toward the hall-way, hoping Michael would appear. He didn't. She could hear Ben upstairs, still calling his dog.

Sophia filled a mug with coffee and set it in front of her, and that was quickly followed by a juice glass, a napkin, a small plate and a knife. "Cream and sugar?"

"Cream, please." Jess was still having trouble keeping up.

Sophia set a small porcelain pitcher on the counter next to Jess's coffee cup, along with a matching pot of jam. "Where did you and Michael meet?"

"We met at a friend's wedding a couple of weeks ago."

"I see." She consulted an open cookbook on the counter. "I hope you like pumpkin pie."

"Definitely."

"Pop! Pop! Poppy!" Ben's voice was getting closer.

A small white dog raced into the room, dog tags jangling on its red sparkly collar. *Please let those be rhinestones.* Michael and his brother were close behind.

"Poppy! See? I have a dog."

"I see that. Is Poppy a boy dog or a girl dog?"

"Girl." Ben scooped her into his arms. "Want to pet her?"

"I'd love to." Jess stroked the fluffy white head.

"Good dog," Ben said.

"She's beautiful. Who looks after her?" Jess asked.

"Me!"

Sophia gently placed her hand on her son's arm. "Ben, please, no shouting in the house."

Ben held a finger to his lips. "Ssshhh. No shouting."

Jess repeated the gesture. "No shouting," she said solemnly. "I'll be good, I promise."

He beamed at her. "I like you. What's your name?"

"My name is Jess."

"Hi, Jessie."

Michael sat on the stool next to Jess and put his arm around her shoulders. "That's Ben's way of saying welcome to the family."

Sophia looked at her and Michael, and Jess could

have sworn her smile was also a stamp of approval. It was more likely the work of an overactive imagination on Jess's part, but she decided she already liked Sophia. A lot.

Michael picked up a scone and took a bite. "You look tired, Mom. I hope you haven't been overdoing things." The concern in his voice was obvious.

So was the defensiveness in Sophia's. "I might not be getting any younger, but I'm doing just fine, thank you very much."

"Good to hear it," he said, then he turned to Jess. "When you've finished your coffee, let's take Ben and Poppy for a walk so my mother can work on her pies."

"Thank you," Sophia said. "Ben, you need to put on your jacket and gloves if you're going for a walk."

"Hot outside. I'm not cold."

"It's not hot, and you will be cold if you don't dress properly."

"Look, Ben. I'm wearing my jacket," Jess said.

"Me, too!" He left the kitchen, apparently satisfied that a jacket was the way to go.

"Thank you." Sophia slid the plate of scones closer to her. "Have something to eat before you go out."

There was no saying no to this woman, so she helped herself to a warm scone, lightly flavored with orange and cinnamon, while Michael devoured a second. "Sophia, this is delicious."

When she finished eating, Michael stood and held out his hand. She put her hand in his, unable to resist touching him, more than a little surprised that he was so openly affectionate, and intensely aware of his mother's scrutiny. To say the past fifteen minutes had been bewildering, overwhelming and totally unexpected would be such an understatement.

"Are you sure you wouldn't like some help?" Jess asked. "I offered to bring something, but Michael said you had dinner covered."

"Dinner is under control, thank you, dear. You run along with Michael and Ben. A little peace and quiet is all the help I need."

Ben had taken his dog outside to wait. He had put on a dark blue hooded jacket and Poppy was on a leash that matched her collar.

"Poppy looks good in red," Jess said to Ben.

"She got diamonds," he said.

"I see that."

Michael reached over a high gate and unlatched it from the other side, and they followed Ben and Poppy into the vineyard.

The sky was overcast but with no threat of rain. The air was heavy with a damp, earthy scent, and it was perfectly still and quiet, except for the sound of birds and Ben's voice as he walked ahead of them, talking to his dog.

"This is amazing," she said. "I wouldn't have thought the vineyard would be so close to the house."

"This is only one of our vineyards," he said. "For as long as I've been involved in the business, we've leased others and bought grapes from several growers in the valley. In the last couple of years we've bought a number of new vineyards, as well."

She tried to think of intelligent-sounding questions to ask about the wine-making business, but she was distracted by Michael's hand on hers, and her head was flooded with the crazy kinds of thoughts a teenager might have when she has a boyfriend for the first time. Which wasn't exactly the case, but it wasn't that far from the truth, either.

When will he kiss me again? Does bringing me to meet his family mean he's serious? Does he really like me? Is he treating me like a girlfriend so I'll sell the Whiskey Sour? Or is he just trying to get me into bed? Oh, God. Sophia had invited her into the kitchen and asked Michael to "take their bags upstairs." Did he assume she would spend the night in *his* room? Is that what his mother expected? Michael had simply said they'd spend the night because dinner would go late and his mother had plenty of room. Judging by the size of the house, she also had plenty of *rooms*. Jess just hoped she'd have one to herself.

She looked up at him, wanting to ask and not knowing how.

"I'm glad you decided to come," he said.

"I'm glad you invited me." All week she'd been having second thoughts about coming here, but Rory and Paige had both said, "Go!" They'd called every day and gradually eroded her misgivings over spending the holiday here with the Morgan family. Rory had even shown up on Wednesday afternoon with an armload of clothes she could borrow.

Jess had insisted she was fine. "I already have the green sweater set and the pink top you gave me."

Rory had been horrified. "He's already seen you in those clothes. You don't want him to think those are the only things you own."

They pretty much were, but according to Rory, he didn't need to know that. Even his mother had been dressed up and she was making a pie, so now Jess was glad she had listened to her friends. Other than those few new items, she really wouldn't have had a thing to wear.

So here she was, decked out in a black-and-white houndstooth car coat with an emerald-green scarf and matching gloves. Okay, the gloves were still in her pocket, but Michael was doing a wonderful job of keeping one hand warm.

"Are all of your vineyards this big?" she asked.

"This is one of the smaller ones, and one of the oldest. These are merlot grapes, which is the wine we're best known for. In the past few years we've bought properties in different parts of the valley because the microclimate and soil type have a lot to do with the variety and quality of the grapes we can produce. I wanted to expand the business, and expanding the types of wine we offered seemed to be the way to go."

He'd obviously been right on the money with that decision, just as he had been with the wine bars. Did he ever make a wrong move? She doubted it. She knew Morgan Estate produced an impressive variety of wines. She had looked into carrying a couple of them in the bar and quickly realized that wouldn't be possible unless she hiked her prices.

"Who's the 'we' you refer to when you talk about all of this?"

"My family, mostly, and we've hired a world-class winemaker. He's been experimenting with some of the new grapes, with excellent results, and we've launched several new wines since he joined us. I hired the best managers I could find for the wine bars—you met Kathryn at the wharf. My sister Ginny—you'll meet her and her husband when they come for dinner—heads up our marketing department. She puts together all of our advertising campaigns, designs all the new labels, that sort of thing."

Ben stopped walking and turned around. "Ginny's baby got lost. Me and Poppy are looking for it."

Jess looked to Michael for clarification.

"He doesn't miss a beat," he said. "That's right, Ben. Ginny and Paul lost their baby." To her, he mouthed the word *miscarriage*.

"I see. I'm sorry to hear that."

"Dogs are good at finding people," Ben said.

"That's what I've been told," Jess said, but she couldn't stop herself from smiling. Poppy, with her fake diamond collar and leash, was as far from being a search-and-rescue dog as a dog could be.

Ben waited for her and Michael to catch up and fell into step next to her. "Hold hands, too?"

"Of course." She took his mittened hand and an odd rush of emotion filled her chest.

The school where she'd been teaching before her grandfather died had a program for students with developmental challenges and she had often thought that working one-on-one with those students would have felt much more rewarding than trying to manage a classroom full of students who didn't want to be there.

"Do you go to school, Ben?"

"No. I stay home. Look after Poppy."

"Good for you. Taking care of someone else is hard work." She wondered if Sophia had help. Michael seemed to understand that his mother needed a break, which was why he had suggested going for a walk, but a woman Sophia's age should have more regular and consistent support than that.

"We'll fix the car?" Ben asked. His out-of-the-blue question interrupted her thoughts.

"Not today," Michael said. "It's a holiday. But when we get back to the house, we can take Jess out to the garage and show it to her."

"Jessie likes cars?"

"I sure do. What kind of car do you have?" she asked.

"Blue," Ben said with authority. "You have a blue car?"

Jess laughed. "No. I have red Vespa."

"That's a car?"

"Not exactly. It's like a motorcycle, only smaller."

"Motorcycles aren't cars."

"No, they're not."

"I like cars. We'll fix the car today?" he asked again, still hopeful.

"We'll take Jess to see your car when we get back to the house," Michael said. For a man with such a go-get-'em approach to business, he had an endless reserve of patience for his brother's frequently repeated questions.

For the next twenty minutes they wandered through the rows of grapevines, pausing from time to time while a blade of grass or some new scent caught the attention of the little dog. Michael had taken the leash, and he and his brother had continued to hold Jess's hands. She didn't want it to end.

Eventually, though, the dog showed signs of tiring and so did Ben. When they returned to the house, the kitchen was spotlessly clean and filled with the spicy aroma of baking pumpkin pies, but there was no sign of Sophia.

"Mom?" Ben yelled the instant they were inside.

Michael shushed him and unclipped Poppy's leash. "She's upstairs resting. Let's go out to the garage." The dog headed straight for her water bowl.

"Show Jessie the car," Ben said.

"Do you mind?" Michael asked.

"Of course not. I remember you telling Larry and Bill about it the first time you came into the Whiskey Sour. I'd like to see it."

Ben rushed down a short hallway off the kitchen, which was more of a mudroom with a laundry room on one side and a powder room on the other—and she and Michael followed. The door at the end opened into a four-car garage.

The space closest to the house was occupied by a nondescript dark gray SUV, most likely Sophia's. The two stalls in the middle were empty. The car in the farthest space was completely concealed by a fitted canvas cover.

Ben helped Michael uncover it and turned to her, as proud as can be. "See my car? It's blue."

Wow. Jess didn't know what to say. Ben's car was a classic open roadster with long sweeping lines, silvery-blue paint and a luxurious-looking red leather interior.

"That's a very cool car, Ben. And it's my favorite shade of blue."

"We fix the car today?" he asked.

"Not today, sport. It's a holiday, remember? That's why Jess is here." Michael put his arm around her. "What do you think of Ben's Morgan?"

"It's gorgeous." She could picture it on the road with him behind the wheel. "My grandfather would have been impressed."

"Jessie wants to fix the car?"

His persistence made her laugh. "I don't know how. Maybe we can find something else to do, though. Do you like to play games?"

"Go Fish!" Ben shouted, and raced for the door to the house. "I'll show you."

"Thanks," Michael said. "You have a knack for creating a distraction."

"I used to be a teacher, remember?"

He caught her before she could leave and pulled her into his arms. "No, I don't think that's it." He kissed her on the forehead. "Must be those green eyes." He kissed her again, this time on the tip of her nose. "Or maybe it's—"

"I thought you were talking about distracting your brother."

He brushed her lips with his. "Who?"

"Behave yourself," she warned. "Otherwise I'll have to keep you after school."

"What would it take to get a whole week's worth of detention?"

"More than a misdemeanor."

He held her face between both his hands and kissed her again, this time with purpose and a little tongue. "Does that qualify?"

She opened her eyes and looked into his. "Definitely."

Apparently satisfied, he let her go. "Go on inside. While I'm out here I'll move my car into the garage. I'll join you in a couple of minutes."

She was still enjoying the afterglow of Michael's kiss when she followed Ben into the house. Sophia was back in the kitchen and Ben was in the family room, hauling games out of a cabinet.

"Did you enjoy your walk?" Sophia asked.

"It's beautiful here. I've never walked through a vineyard before. It seems to go on forever."

"Wait till you see it in the spring when the vines are turning green. That's always been my favorite time of year."

More than anything, Jess hoped she'd be back here in the spring.

Sophia slipped her hands into a pair of oven mitts. "My daughter Ginny called while you were out with the boys. She and Paul are leaving soon and should be here in half an hour or so."

"I'm looking forward to meeting them."

"It's too bad Lexi couldn't be here for the holiday. She said she had to fly down to L.A. on business." Sophia opened the oven and took out a pie, adding to the already holiday-scented kitchen. "Who does business on Thanksgiving?"

Jess had no idea. "I hope to meet her some other time."

"Oh, you haven't met her already? She lives in the city, too, so I assumed the two of you already knew each other."

Jess couldn't begin to guess what Michael had told his mother about them, but Sophia seemed certain that they were having a relationship, and that they had been having one for more than a couple of weeks. Jess still wasn't convinced there was a relationship at all, unless she counted Michael's interest in the Whiskey Sour.

"Mikey! Jessie! Play *this* game!" Ben shouted when Michael joined them.

Sophia put her fingers to her lips. "Inside voices, remember?" she said quietly.

Ben imitated her. "Ssshhh."

"Thank you. Now show Michael and Jess which game you'd like to play."

"This one!" He smacked a hand on the Trivial Pursuit box.

"That one's too hard for me," Jess said. "I thought you wanted to play Go Fish."

He grabbed a much smaller box and held it up so she could see it. "This one!"

"That's more like it."

Ben plunked himself on the floor by the coffee table in the family room. Jess sat cross-legged on the carpet and Michael sprawled on the opposite side of the table, legs stretched to one side.

"Would you like to deal?" he asked Ben.

Ben shook his head vigorously. "Jessie deals," he said and handed the cards to her.

She laughed and slid the deck out of the box. "All right, but I'm warning you. I'm a bit of a card shark."

"I'll win," Ben said.

Michael winked at her. "He's right. He always does."

The night she met him he had given the impression that he excelled at whatever he did, and he liked to win. She had a competitive streak, too, so she had been able to relate to it. This was a different side of Michael, an unexpected one, and she liked it.

"How many cards should I deal to each player?" she asked Ben.

"Five." He held up one hand, showing all five fingers.

"Very good." The cards were large and made from

stiff, heavy board, perfect for even the least coordinated hands. She carefully counted as she dealt them so Ben could follow along then set the remaining cards face-down in the middle of the table.

"Me first," Ben said. "Mikey has a bunny?"

Jess stifled a giggle. He was so *not* a Mikey, although he looked awfully adorable, sitting there with the over-size, brightly colored cards fanned out in one hand.

He shot her a warning look and handed a rabbit card to his brother. Ben matched the two cards and set them on the table. "See? I'm winning."

Twenty minutes later, as predicted, Ben was declared the Go Fish champion. Sophia coaxed the conquering hero into the kitchen for a snack while Michael and Jess put away the cards and the other games Ben had dragged out of the cabinet. A framed photograph on a shelf above caught Jesse's attention—the only family photo in the room that she could see. Michael, smiling, maybe sixteen or seventeen and the embodiment of every teenage girl's dream, was posed with his brother and his sisters. The elder of the two girls, who looked about thirteen, was proudly holding baby Ben. That had to be Ginny. The younger girl, Lexi, was turned away from the camera, tickling the baby's chin with the end of one long dark braid.

Like so many things lately, it reminded Jess of her childhood, one that had been devoid of family photographs, among other things. She shook off the feeling and looked away.

A sound from the front of the house caught Ben's attention and, snack forgotten, he ran out of the room. "Ginny!"

"As you can see, he's our welcoming committee,"

Sophia said. "He loves it when his family comes home."

As much as Sophia loved having them home, Jess thought. She stifled the momentary rush of bitterness she felt toward her own mother for never making the holidays special. Then Michael pulled her into a quick hug that made it easy to let go of the past.

Chapter Ten

The Morgan family's Thanksgiving dinner was a lively affair, served in the large dining room. Like everything else in the house, the furniture looked expensive but inviting—a blend of West Coast casual and old Italian villa. The light from an ornate wrought-iron chandelier cast a warm glow over the table that had been set with simple gold-rimmed white china and sparkling crystal. The centerpiece—a long shallow basket filled with pillar candles, tiny orange pumpkins, autumn-colored squashes and assorted greenery—was perfect for the holiday.

Michael uncorked the wine as Jess and Ginny helped Sophia carry steaming platters and bowls of food to the table. All day he had been charming and attentive, and that continued during dinner. Sophia had arranged for Jess to sit on one side of the table between him and Ben. Ginny and her husband, Paul, sat across from them.

"I can't image what's so important in L.A. that couldn't have waited till next week," Sophia said, gazing at the vacant space next to Ginny where Lexi should have been sitting.

Michael's mother was an amazing cook, and Jess was glad that she hadn't been expected to contribute anything. Her kitchen was poorly equipped and her cooking skills weren't that great anyway. Anything she could have prepared would not have measured up, and something from the deli would not have gone over well.

Michael and his sister seemed to have a great connection, especially where the family business was concerned, but Sophia shushed them when the conversation shifted to work. "No business at dinnertime," she reminded them. "Especially not on a holiday."

Ginny was a petite and stunningly beautiful dynamo, a younger version of her mother. She had ideas and opinions about everything, and she wasn't afraid to express them. She declined the wine Michael offered her, saying she'd had a touch of flu and wasn't feeling great.

The one thing they all had in common was their devotion and protectiveness toward Ben. He was good-natured, thrived on being the center of attention, and it was clear that he was well provided for and much loved. She couldn't help thinking, though, that he had been a little too sheltered, and that maybe he could benefit from getting out in the world a little more.

Not that it's any of your business, she reminded herself. Still, although she hadn't worked with kids with developmental challenges, she'd seen young adults like Ben who were far more self-sufficient.

Clinking glasses was a long-standing family tradition, it seemed, and one that Ben especially loved. As a result, there was a great deal of toasting and general revelry at dinnertime and, with a glass of grape juice gripped firmly in his hand, he had been the most enthusiastic participant. While Sophia presided from one end of the table, the chair at the other opposite end was noticeably empty. One of the many toasts was to Michael's father, and everyone raised their glasses in that direction. It had been done with a lot of respect and a lot of love, and Jess admired a family that honored the people they'd lost. That was exactly what she was trying to do for her grandfather, so it shouldn't be hard for Michael to understand why the Whiskey Sour wasn't for sale.

After Sophia's delicious pumpkin pie was served and eaten, Jess was wishing the meal would never end. It had been a perfect evening in the company of a perfect family. She would never find the words to tell Michael how much she loved being there, but she would find a way to thank him.

THE HOUSE WAS AS QUIET after dinner as it had been hectic during the festivities. Ginny and Paul left after the dishes had been cleared away and his mother had gone upstairs with Ben to get him settled for the night. Michael looked in the study to see if Jess was there, but she wasn't. He wandered through the kitchen and family room, then saw her outside, resting her forearms on the top edge of the stone wall that separated the terrace from the vineyard.

She was wearing slim-fitting black pants and a dark moss-green sweater that matched her eyes perfectly, and her hair was in a ponytail. She had long, thick, extravagantly red hair that begged to be touched, and he'd like to see her let it down more often, the way she'd worn it last Saturday evening. He'd have to work on that.

All day he'd found himself thinking back to Lexi's warning, that he couldn't "have it all," but now he was becoming more and more convinced that's what he wanted. Jess was having trouble keeping her business afloat and if she would give his offer some serious consideration, she would see it was the perfect solution. There was also no denying that he and Jess had a connection, and he was ready to explore that to its logical conclusion.

He watched her hug herself and wondered if she was cold. Maybe he should take a jacket to her.

No. He knew a better way to keep her warm.

He poured two glasses of wine and carried them outside. "Here you are." He held out one glass. "I've been looking for you."

She accepted it without looking at him. "Thank you."

"Are you okay?"

She nodded and set the glass on the stone ledge, untouched.

He could tell she wasn't. "Did someone say something to make you uncomfortable? If they did—"

"No," she said quickly. "Not at all. Your family's great."

He set down his own glass. "Then tell me what's going on." He hooked his forefinger under her chin so she had to look up at him. Her eyes looked suspiciously moist. "What is it?"

"It's nothing anyone did. It's just me. I've..." Her voice had developed an uncharacteristic waver. "I'm being silly, I know, but I..." She paused again and took a deep breath. "This might sound crazy, but until today I've never had a real family Thanksgiving dinner."

During those few seconds while he waited for her response, he'd considered several possible explanations for her unexpected withdrawal. Like maybe his mother had asked if she ever planned to have children, or Ginny had told her about the women he usually dated. But he couldn't have imagined this, not in a million years. And now she was shivering and one the verge of tears.

"Come here." He drew her back against his chest, wrapped his arms around her waist and held her close. He didn't know what to say, couldn't imagine what she needed to hear, but this he could do. She gradually relaxed, and as her slender body settled back against his, his body reacted. *Tonight is not the night,* he reminded himself. But he drew her a little closer anyway. He picked up her glass and handed it to her, then he picked up his own and touched it to hers. "Thank you," he said.

She tipped her head back slightly and looked up at him. "For what?"

"For reminding me that I need to appreciate what I have. I've always lived here and it's always been like this. For a lot of years when I was growing up, I assumed everyone lived this way. It's easy to take it all for granted, and I shouldn't. I'm sorry if that's what has upset you."

"I'm not upset, and don't get me wrong. Granddad did what he could to make the holiday special. We'd spruce up the place with pumpkins and paper cutouts of Pilgrim hats, and in those days when Eric's dad was our cook, we'd have roasted turkey sandwiches and pumpkin pie on the menu and the place was always busy."

Michael tried to imagine Thanksgiving in a tackily decorated bar full of strangers, drinking beer and eating turkey sandwiches. It was easier to imagine a shuttle flight to the space station. "It sounds…" It sounded awful, but he couldn't say that.

"I'm not complaining," she said, taking a sip of her

wine. "I knew it wasn't a traditional Thanksgiving. When I was in college, friends used to invite me to go home with them for the holidays, but I always wanted to spend it with him. I still miss him."

The nubbly texture of her sweater was soft beneath the palm of his hand where it rested just beneath her breasts. He was tempted to move his hand higher, just to see how far she'd let him go, but he resisted. Then she put her hand over his and he held his breath, wondering if she would push his away. She didn't. She laced her fingers with his, which meant he couldn't move his hand. On the plus side, it meant he didn't have to.

Having her here today felt so completely right. It was as if she belonged here in his home, with his family, with him, and he would gladly stand here with her in his arms all night if that's what she needed. "I wish I could have met your grandfather."

"You would have liked him. He wasn't a high-powered businessman, but he had a way with people."

Was that how she saw him? A high-powered businessman? Last week he had called Larry, one of the mechanics he'd met the first time he dropped by the bar to see her, to order a part for the old Morgan. Larry had called the next day to say he'd found it, so Michael had made arrangements to pick it up. It hadn't taken much to get Larry talking about his old friend. Sam Bennett had been a hardworking family man who had never come to terms with having a daughter who ran wild. His granddaughter had lived up to his expectations, though, and there had been nothing he wouldn't do for her.

"Did you have a busy week at the bar?" he asked.

"Not as busy as last Saturday night, which is too bad, because I need to hire a plumber."

Lexi had mentioned something about a plumbing disaster after she'd paid the place a visit. "I can get one of my managers to recommend someone if you'd like."

"As long as he…or she…works cheap," Jess said. "And fast. Someone from the health department is hounding me to get it fixed."

Hmm. Was Lexi behind that? Of course she was. But Jess would never find out, he reminded himself. Besides, they were doing her a favor.

"Granddad used to fix those kinds of things himself," she said. "Now it's just me and Eric, and neither of us has a clue about building maintenance."

That he could believe, he thought, smiling at the recollection of Eric fixing Jess's hair the night he'd taken her out to dinner. Michael had seen her in action at the bar, though, and there she was in her element. Great with customers—probably a lot like her grandfather in that regard—but without a head for business. Or plumbing.

"I've applied for a bank loan so I can do some work on the building. My grandfather devoted his life to that place and I have to keep it going, to honor his memory. Like the way you're doing for your father and grandfather," she said. "The Whiskey Sour is nothing like this, but it's the only real home I've ever had. This might sound silly, but it's like part of him is still there. If I can't keep it together, I'll lose that connection to my granddad, and then I won't have anything."

Michael was blindsided. He held her a little closer, enjoying the feel of her in his arms, the sweet scent of her mingling with the fresh night air, and realized, for the first time since he'd met her, that they had a lot more in common than he'd ever imagined.

What she'd said about her grandfather was *exactly* how he felt about his father when he stepped into the den. Every time he walked through one of the original winery buildings, it was as if his grandfather's spirit was there with him. No matter how big the company became, those places would never change. Not as long as he was in charge.

Could he take that away from Jess and still live with himself? Not a chance. In the space of a few seconds he knew what he had to do. On Monday he'd make an offer on the Folsom Street building, and when he met with Lexi in the afternoon he'd tell her the plan had changed and that she needed to back off. Then he'd figure out a way to help Jess.

She yawned.

"Sleepy?"

"I am."

"We've had a long day," he said. "We should get to bed."

The words slipped out before he could catch them. He could tell from the way her body went rigid that she thought he meant something other than he intended. He set his wineglass on the wall, then put his arm around her again and pressed his mouth against her ear. "Remember when I told you that the first time I make love to a woman, I like it to be in a bed?" he whispered, absolutely certain that would get a reaction from her. He was right.

She swung around to face him, her eyes dark and challenging, and she tried to wriggle out of his arms.

He held her close. "News flash," he said, trying not to smile and failing badly. "That bed is *not* in my mother's house, so I'm afraid you're out of luck. Not here. Not tonight. I just meant that we should get some sleep."

"Oh." She lowered her gaze and tried to move away. "Sorry."

He kept his arms around her. "No, I'm the one who has to apologize. I shouldn't have baited you. Besides, it's not like the idea hadn't crossed my mind."

She looked up at him, and even in the dim outdoor lighting on the terrace he could see the uncertainty in her eyes. But now there was something else, too. It could be wishful thinking on his part, but he was getting the message that she was coming around to acknowledging her own needs, that she was getting close to wanting this as much as he did.

And now that all their cards were on the table, what was stopping him from kissing her? Nothing. So he did.

At first the taste of her mingled on his tongue with the wine, and having her in his arms, kissing her, felt absolutely right. Jess's arms snaked around his neck and the rest of her melted against him, and all of a sudden kissing her felt like a mistake because he didn't want to stop there. Jess's body language was saying she didn't, either. If he was going to make a mistake, it might as well be a big one.

He slipped a hand under her sweater and stroked the warm skin on her back. She moved a little closer and her hips connected with his. His body ached for her touch.

"You're amazing," he whispered against her mouth.

She opened her eyes and looked into his. "I am?"

"You are." And he looked forward to convincing her that she was.

He had wanted his family to meet her, wanted to see how she reacted to Ben, whether seeing the house and the winery would bring out the latent gold digger in her. It hadn't.

This was the first time he'd invited a woman to spend the night here and going to bed alone, knowing she was under his roof and just down the hall, so close and unattainable, was going to kill him.

Her laughter was soft and contagious. They were still laughing when they carried their empty wineglasses back inside. He took hers and put them both in the dishwasher. "Come on. I'll walk you to your room."

He kissed her good-night at the door of the guest room. It wasn't the kind of kiss that would get something started. They both knew better than to go there now. This was a comfortable kiss between two people who liked each other and were happy with where they were in their relationship.

"Good night," she said.

"See you in the morning."

Their relationship. He thought about that some more as he walked to his bedroom. For the first time in a long time—no, it was really the first time ever, he felt as if he was in a relationship. He enjoyed spending time with her, liked her forthrightness, appreciated her natural beauty and uncontrived style. He wanted to make love to her more than any woman he'd ever met, and yet he was in no real hurry to take that step. When it happened he knew it would be amazing, but he wanted it to be the best sex she'd ever had. For that to happen she had to trust him. She was starting to trust him, and he wouldn't do anything to jeopardize that. By Monday morning, he would have a plan to save the Whiskey Sour for her and that, he was certain, would seal the deal.

Chapter Eleven

On Monday morning Jess was at the bar well before opening time to look after the deliveries and go over the accounts. It was her least favorite part of the job, but it had to be done. She put on a pot of coffee and leaned on the bar as she sorted receipts and bills into piles while she waited for the machine to stop sputtering.

"I hate bookkeeping," she said out loud, even though there was no one to hear her. "And I hate money." No, what she hated was not having money. She poured herself a cup of coffee and tried to concentrate on the paperwork spread across the bar. Instead, she studied a narrow crack in the ancient granite countertop for a few seconds, trying to recall what had been dropped on it, then ran her fingertips across the polished surface. Her grandfather had leaned on this counter, spilled drinks on it and wiped it clean thousands of times. She intended to do the same.

"As soon as I've finished calculating how much money I don't have, I'll call the bank." They had to come through. They just had to.

One good thing—the *only* good thing—about being a teacher had been the steady paycheck, and it had seemed like a good career move until she'd become the sole adult in a roomful of teenagers. She'd had terrible classroom management skills, which meant the kids were frequently out of control. For someone like her, who needed to be in control at all times, it had been a nightmare.

Maybe she would have enjoyed teaching if she'd worked with kids like Ben. He had given her a big hug when they'd left to return to the city the day after Thanksgiving. Michael had openly admitted to testing her by not telling her about Ben before she met him, and Sophia had hinted that Jess was the first woman in Michael's life to form an immediate bond with his brother. That brought her thoughts around to the real reason she was finding it hard to concentrate on the miserable books. She wanted to replay, for at least the hundredth time, every moment of the Morgan family's celebration.

Even when she was a young kid, she had known her mother simply didn't have what it took to keep a family together. Not even a family of two. Roxanne Bennett was inclined to scrimp on groceries and buy a skimpy new dress instead, with the hope of attracting a man who would put food on the table. There had been no shortage of men, but the table had often been bare. Jess used to imagine what it would be like to have a mother who had breakfast on the table before her kid went to school and who was there with a glass of milk and a plate of homemade cookies when she got home.

Sophia Morgan was that mother. She had a home worthy of a magazine spread, and yet it was warm, welcoming, lived-in. She had prepared a gourmet holiday feast for her family and made it look effortless. She was proud of all her children—and justifiably so—and she doted on Ben. Jess suspected she put her own needs last, but that was infinitely better than always putting them first.

Michael's sister Ginny was in charge of marketing for Morgan Estate, and by all accounts was doing an outstanding job. She had treated Jess like a member of the family and right away she'd seemed exactly like the kind of big sister Jess had always wanted—someone who was well-grounded and as family-oriented as her mother. The mother in question being Sophia Morgan, not Roxanne Bennett. If two mothers could possibly be more different, Jess couldn't imagine how that might be.

Michael's other sister Lexi, whom she had yet to meet, was an architect with a rapidly expanding business in San Francisco. She had designed the wine bars at Fisherman's Wharf and on Nob Hill, and was currently working on an expansion at the winery. During dinner, when Jess had mentioned her plan to renovate the Whiskey Sour, Sophia had urged her to talk to Lexi, because she was "the best in the business." Jess wouldn't have been quick to accept a mother's endorsement if she hadn't already been to their Fisherman's Wharf location and seen Lexi's talents firsthand.

Ben had stolen her heart the instant she met him. He adored his older brother, a feeling that was clearly mutual. She loved that he called him Mikey, and while Jessie had always been her least favorite nickname for Jessica, having Ben add *ie* to the end of her name had really made her feel like part of the family.

And then there was Michael. At first she had thought he was interested in her only because he wanted to buy the Whiskey Sour, but he hadn't disappeared when he found out it wasn't for sale. Then she'd thought he wanted only to get her into bed, but even that impression was short-lived. Now she was still having trouble wrapping her mind around the idea that a man like him wanted to spend time with a woman like her, but on many levels they seemed—did she even dare to entertain the idea?— compatible. In spite of his money and success, he was grounded and practical, he was all about family, he was heart-meltingly sexy…and he was willing to wait until she got past her hang-ups around sexual intimacy. Had he meant what he'd said about being willing to wait? Time would tell.

She paper-clipped a wad of receipts together, drained her coffee cup and refilled it. Eric arrived just as she was heading to her office. He had agreed to come in early because Michael had invited her to join him for lunch at Morgan's on Nob Hill, saying they had something to celebrate, although he hadn't said what that was.

"How's it going?" Eric asked, eyeing the wad of papers in her hand.

"We're not broke yet. One of the suppliers delivered a couple of kegs this morning and they still have to be moved into the keg room. Would you mind taking care of that while I enter this stuff in the computer?"

"No problem." He tossed his jacket onto the back of a bar stool. "Is that what you're wearing to lunch?"

Oh, dear God. "What's wrong with this?" She was wearing her black dress pants and yet another of the beautiful sweaters Rory had let her borrow for the weekend. This one was a brick-red turtleneck with black edging on the collar and cuffs.

Eric grinned. "Nothing wrong. Just asking."

Just pushing her buttons was more like it. "Get to work or you'll be looking for a new job."

He disappeared into the basement, laughing, just as the phone rang.

Who could that be? Both Rory and Paige had already called, wanting to hear all the details about Thanksgiving in Napa Valley. There had already been a "courtesy call" from the telephone company with a reminder that last month's bill was still outstanding. As if she needed to be reminded.

"Please don't be another bill collector," she said to the phone. "Or the health inspector." She let it ring a couple of times, debating whether or not to answer.

Maybe it's Michael.

She grabbed it before the answering machine kicked in. "The Whiskey Sour. This is Jess."

"Miss Bennett?"

Crap. It was a woman's voice, and a formal-sounding one at that.

"Speaking."

"Good morning. It's Pamela Robbins, Mr. Taylor's assistant."

Finally, a call from the bank. She'd been starting to think they'd lost her application. She closed her eyes and crossed the fingers of one hand, hoping for the best, but fully prepared to hear the worst.

We're happy to tell you that your loan application has been approved and you can have all the money you want. Ha.

We're very sorry. You have a lousy credit rating and your loan application has been denied.

On the bright side, it wasn't someone asking *her* for money.

"I'm calling about your loan application."

Of course you are. Greg Taylor had been personable and professional, but he would have better things to do than call and tell some no-account bartender that her loan application had been turned down.

"Mr. Taylor asked me to call and let you know he can't make a final decision until we see a copy of your building permit. Can you drop that off today?"

Crap. "I'll see what I can do," she said. After she hung up, she stared at the phone while she hastily formulated a plan, then she gathered up her paperwork and calculator and dumped then on the desk in the office.

"Eric?" she called from the top of the stairs.

"Yeah?"

"Can you come up for a sec? It's important."

Eric dashed up from the keg room. "What's wrong? Don't tell me that bloody toilet—"

"The toilet is fine." Knock on wood. "It's the bank. Somebody just called and—"

A slow smile spread across his face. "About the loan? You got it?"

"I wish," she said, shaking her head. "It hasn't been approved yet because they haven't seen the building permit. I've called the city about it twice and they keep giving me the runaround, so I'm going to leave now and go there in person before I meet Michael for lunch."

"What's the holdup, I wonder? Do you think it's the plumbing? Maybe they won't issue a permit until you've been cleared by the health department."

Hmm. She hadn't considered that. "I told them I need the building permit to get the loan, and I need the loan to fix the plumbing." How much simpler could it be?

"Then you'd better get going. It's harder for them to

say no in person than it is over the phone. I'll hold down the fort."

She hugged him. "I don't know what I'd do without you. I'll see you after lunch. I don't know how long this will take. If Michael calls, can you tell him where I am and that I'll be there as quick as I can?"

"Of course." He gave her a gentle shove toward the door and a playful swat on the rear. "Now, get out of here. And don't take no for an answer."

JESS HADN'T TAKEN no for an answer, but she still hadn't heard yes, either. What was that old saying? You can't fight city hall? No kidding. She now had proof that you couldn't even reason with it. She had eventually left with the knowledge that her permit was still under consideration, but no one could tell her when it might be issued. Michael had a lot more experience with this sort of thing—maybe he'd have some advice.

She still had plenty of time before she met him for lunch, so she took a somewhat circuitous route to the wine bar on Nob Hill. The Vespa was great in the city, just not on the really steep hills. She arrived with fifteen minutes to spare, which was a lucky thing because finding a parking spot proved challenging, even for a small bike. She finally tucked it into a space for passenger drop-off only and hoped there wouldn't be a ticket waiting for her when lunch was over. She pulled off her helmet, took a quick look at her hair in the little sideview mirror, then smoothed it out and walked down the block.

The plate-glass doors at the entrance to Morgan's on Nob Hill were identical to those at Morgan's at the Wharf, and the name arched across the two doors was in the same gold lettering. She pulled one open and stepped into the marble-floored foyer. A young woman in a subdued black dress welcomed her from the hostess station.

"Hi," Jess said. "I'm meeting Michael for lunch."

The young woman smiled graciously. "Of course. He called to say he was running a little late, but he'll be here as soon as he can and that if you arrived before he did, I should show you to your table."

She glanced at Jess's windbreaker and the helmet tucked under her arm. "Would you like me to take those for you?"

"No, that's okay. I'll hang on to them." She followed the woman to a table in a secluded alcove, separated from the hostess station by a wood-paneled planter filled with potted palms.

"Would you like a glass of wine while you wait?"

"Thanks, but I'll wait for Michael." She had no idea what to order and he most likely had something in mind.

"Of course. I'll get you some ice water."

"Thanks." She hung her jacket on the back of her chair, tucked her helmet under her seat and took in her surroundings. There were lots of similarities between this place and the one at the wharf—the rich, dark wood, the cream-colored table linens, even the bud vases on each table. The artwork was by a different artist, more traditional in style, but she had no doubt the paintings were originals. But where the view from Morgan's at the Wharf incorporated all the hustle and bustle of the waterfront, Morgan's on Nob Hill had a hushed atmosphere, like a library, further emphasized by one long wall lined with book-laden shelves. It would be interesting to see how Michael would integrate the "signature Morgan experience" with the new place in SoMa.

She could see the entrance through the palm fronds, which meant that when he came in, she would see him before he noticed her. And there was no question that she was looking forward to seeing him. Now that she had convinced herself that he wasn't trying to buy the Whiskey Sour, it seemed that he really was interested in her. Her! As unbelievable as it was, Jess Bennett had caught the attention of a deliciously handsome, successful family man, and she was already a little bit in love with him.

Her ice water arrived and she took a few sips while watching the entrance. Several more minutes ticked by, and then a tall woman in a business suit came in. She looked familiar, but it took a few seconds for Jess to remember why. It was the mystery woman who'd come into the Whiskey Sour a few weeks ago and ordered a beer and a panini for lunch. This place seemed much more her style.

"Hi, Lexi," the hostess said. "I thought you were meeting with Michael later this afternoon."

Lexi? Michael's sister? What a bizarre coincidence.

She set her briefcase on the floor. "I was supposed to, but my flight from L.A. was late and now something's come up with another project. I have to do a site visit not far from here, so I thought I'd drop this off on my way." She handed a large, sturdy-looking cardboard tube to the hostess. "These are the plans for the winery expansion. Can you please make sure he gets them?"

"Of course. Would you like to have lunch while you're here?"

"Not today, thanks. I have to get going." The tinny

sound of classical music grabbed her attention. "That's my phone. I'll just take this call, then I have to go."

Jess watched her pick up her briefcase and fish her phone from an exterior pocket. "Lexi Morgan." She cast a furtive glance around the foyer and moved away from the front desk, obviously seeking privacy while being completely unaware that Jess was sitting on the opposite side of the potted palms.

"Yes, that's right," she said, her voice now hushed. "It's a little bar called the Whiskey Sour."

For a second, maybe two, Jess thought she must be mistaken. Lexi had no reason to be talking about her bar with anyone. But then Jess heard her give the address. No mistake about it.

"She applied for a building permit last week and I'm wondering if you could do me a favor...yes, of course, just between you and me...no, I'm not asking you to lose the application, but if you could move it to the bottom of the pile...yeah, keep stalling it as long as you can... sure, okay, thanks. I owe you one."

Jess's heartbeat pounded in her ears, making her dizzy and slightly nauseated, and she had to struggle to take a breath. Oh, God. All the horrible things that had happened in her past suddenly paled compared to the betrayal she felt at that moment.

Lexi tucked her phone back into her bag.

Jess ducked behind the menu. She could confront Lexi right then and there, but it was clear that Michael's sister wasn't acting on her own. She was using her connections to do her brother's dirty work. The phone call about the expired business license, the health inspector showing up to inspect the washrooms, right after Lexi had been there—it all made sense.

Michael's sister waved at the hostess and left.

Jess felt as if she was frozen to her chair. The son of a bitch had really played her. *How dare he?* What gave him the right to interfere with her business? To lie about being interested in her? Wanting to buy the building was one thing, but the phony seduction routine? That was beyond despicable.

You have to get out of here, she told herself. He would be here any minute and she couldn't face him. Not right now. She grabbed her jacket and picked up her helmet, knocking her ice water all over the table in the process. That immediately got the hostess's attention. Jess ignored the startled woman and rushed past her.

All his shmarmy sweet talk about waiting to make love to her until she was ready and...oh, God! She had fallen for it. The other night she had curled up in bed in his mother's guest room and dared to dream that someday she might actually be part of a real family. *His* family. She had let herself believe she was the kind of woman he was genuinely interested in, and had imagined what being in his bed would be like. Worst of all, she had acknowledged that she might even be falling in love with him, and that the feeling was mutual.

She shoved the heavy plate-glass door open and stormed out onto the sidewalk, wishing she had a cell phone so she could call Mr. Hotshot Morgan and tell him to go to hell and take his money with him. Then she'd hang up and never speak to him again.

You are such an idiot! She wanted to scream. And then she wanted to smash something. Something really, really expensive. No, something fragile, like a king-size, arrogant male ego. And then she wanted to curl up in a little ball and cry her eyes out. But first she had to get back to the Whiskey Sour. She ran up the sidewalk, her vision blurred by tears, strapped on her helmet and climbed onto her Vespa. She wished it was a Harley-Davidson, because she was ready to rumble. Instead, she scooted away from the curb as fast as fifty ccs allowed.

MICHAEL WALKED the five blocks from his apartment building to the wine bar. After his morning meetings with the Realtor, the bank and his lawyer, Jonathan, he was looking forward to having lunch with Jess and celebrating the acquisition of his newest property—the building on Folsom Street. He also had ideas for the Whiskey Sour that he wanted to share with her. He couldn't remember the last time he'd felt this excited about a project, and it wasn't even his. He wished he'd been able to track Lexi down, tell her the plan had changed and run his ideas by her first, but that could wait till they met later that afternoon.

A block and half from the restaurant he spotted Jess on her little red scooter. Vespa, he corrected. They looked as cute together as he'd known they would. She didn't look as though she was arriving, though. More as if she was leaving. That was strange. He was only a few minutes late and he had called and asked Cindy, the hostess, to be sure to let Jess know he was on his way. He picked up his pace, but by the time he got to the entrance to Morgan's, she had disappeared.

Inside, Cindy and one of the servers were clearing the table he'd asked them to reserve for him. "Was Jess Bennett here?" he asked.

"She was, but she left a couple of minutes ago. She

must've been in a hurry, because she spilled a glass of water all over the table and ran out the door."

Michael tried to process that information and failed. "Did she say where she was going?"

Cindy bundled the table linens under her arm and walked back to the hostess station with him, leaving the server to reset the table. "No, she didn't say. I thought maybe she got a phone call or something."

That wasn't it. Jess didn't have a cell phone.

"Oh, Lexi was here and left this for you." She handed him an architect's drawing tube. "I think she said it's for the winery."

He knew exactly what it was. What he didn't know was why she'd dropped it off when they had a meeting scheduled for this afternoon.

"She said she has to do a site visit and couldn't meet with you after all."

Okay, that didn't surprise him. With Lexi, things like this happened all the time. But it didn't explain why Jess had rushed out. Unless…damn it…maybe it did. "Was Jess here when Lexi arrived."

"Yes, she was. She was already at your table."

"Did they see each other? Talk to each other?"

Cindy shook her head. "Lexi was only here for a couple of minutes. She gave me the drawings, then she took a call on her cell and then she left."

"And Jess was still here?"

"Yes, but she left right after Lexi did."

That had to be it. Jess had recognized his sister from her visit to the Whiskey Sour and jumped to conclusions. The wrong ones. Now the million-dollar question—had she talked to Lexi after she left? He sure as hell hoped not, because he hadn't told Lexi about the change of plans. Damn it. He hadn't been able to reach her by phone and he hadn't wanted to put it in an email or text message. Not that they'd been doing anything wrong. Technically.

"Thanks, Cindy." He carried the drawing tube and his briefcase into his office and closed the door. The first thing he needed to do was get in touch with his sister. While he counted the rings, he slid his laptop out of his bag and turned it on. "Come on, Lex. Pick up."

"Lexi Morgan."

"Lex, hi. It's Michael."

"Hi, did you get the drawings?"

"Yes. Did you talk to Jess when you were here?"

"No, I didn't even know she was there."

He explained Jess's hasty departure.

"Shit," she said.

"Excuse me?"

"She probably heard me talking on the phone."

"Talking to…?"

"Someone I know in the planning department about, um…" She lowered her voice. "Stalling her building permit application."

And all she could say was shit? He could think of any of number of expletives that were more apt than that. This was a million times worse than Jess simply recognizing his sister. Damn it. She had overheard Lexi on the phone.

"Listen, Michael. I told you from the get-go that this could end badly and you wouldn't listen."

She had, and he hadn't. Now what?

"I'm sorry, Michael, I really am, but you can't put this all on me. You wanted that building and you kept saying this was just business. How was I supposed to know you were going to fall in love with her?"

"I am not in love with her." That was not what this was about.

"Of course you are. You've already taken her home to meet Mom."

He slumped into the chair behind his desk. "To meet Ben, actually. I wanted to see how she was with him."

"And?"

"She was amazing, and he took to her right away. It was…" He couldn't say it out loud, but it was perfect.

"Like it was meant to be?" Lexi's soft laugh wafted into his ear. "Okay, here's the thing. I put my ass on the line at city hall over this. When you decided to go after her instead of the bar, why the hell didn't you tell me?"

"I was going to talk to you when we met this afternoon. I shouldn't have waited."

"No kidding."

"Is there a way to fix this?"

He heard her sigh. "I'm sure there is. What do you want me to do?"

"I talked to people at the bank this morning about arranging financing for her—"

"You're giving her money?"

"I'm helping her get a loan and I was going to ask you if there's a way to fast-track her application for a building permit."

"Does she know about this?"

"Not yet."

"Oh. My. God. You're one of the smartest people I know, and you don't have a clue how this works."

"What are you talking about?" He knew exactly what

he was doing. He could have Jess's bank loan lined up by the end of the day if necessary.

"I'm talking about you and women. First you decide the best thing *for her* is to sell the bar and you set out to make that happen. Then you decide the best thing *for her* is to keep the bar, so you come up with a plan to make that happen. Do you see the flaw in this?"

He leaned back in his chair and ran a hand through his hair. He didn't dare say no.

"Yep, clueless," she said. "You can offer to help and let her make a decision. You can't just do these things and expect her to go along with them."

Oh, hell. She was right. He thought he'd given this a lot of consideration, but he hadn't. At least, he hadn't considered what Jess's reaction might be. Did he always do this? He thought that most of his trouble with women had stemmed from what they did or didn't do. Maybe not. May it was time he did a little soul-searching. Right now Lexi was waiting for his response. "Fine. You're right. I'm clueless. How do I fix this?"

"Have you talked to her? Tried to explain?"

"No. I wanted to know if she had talked to you."

He heard Lexi sigh. "There's no point in calling her. There's no way she'll talk to either of us on the phone. I'll be tied up here for an hour or two, then I can run over there."

"I can do that."

"Honestly, bro. There's a good possibility you've blown it with her. If you let me be the bad guy, maybe she'll give you a second chance."

"You'd do that for me?"

"Oh, don't flatter yourself. I'm not doing this for you—I'm doing it for her."

"Call me after you've seen her?"

"Sure. And you *do* owe me, you know. Big-time."

"What? You want me to take your car to the car wash?" Lexi had found it impossible to stay out of trouble when she was a teenager, and he had usually been the one to smooth things over with their parents. *You owe me,* he used to tell her. *Big-time.* In those days the payoff had been having a car that was always washed, waxed and detailed.

"This is way bigger than helping me cook up an excuse for breaking curfew," she said. "I think you might actually have to buy me a car wash."

She laughed, but part of him was thinking that if she could convince Jess to give him another chance, the car wash was hers.

Right after he ended the call, his phone rang and Ginny's number came up on the display.

"Hi, Ginny. What's happening?"

"Well, I have some good news and I have some bad news."

His thoughts immediately went to the last time he'd got one of these calls from her. "Are you okay? Is Paul there with you?"

"It's not me—I'm fine. It's Mom."

Oh, no. "What happened?"

"She called this morning and said she wasn't feeling well, so I drove over to see her. She looked terrible and she was in a lot of pain, so I called an ambulance. She has a ruptured appendix and she's having surgery this afternoon."

Just what he needed. One more thing to feel guilty about. "I thought she looked tired when we were there on the weekend. I should have said something."

"The doctor says there's nothing anyone could have done to prevent this. They'll keep her in the hospital for a couple of days…maybe just overnight if the surgery goes well…and then she'll need to take it easy for about six weeks."

Good luck with that, he thought, running a hand across the top of his head. "What about Ben? How's he handling this?"

"About as well as you'd expect. He was freaked out when he saw her on the stretcher, and he didn't want the paramedics to take her away. After they left, we drove over to the hospital, and that scared him even more."

"Poor kid. Are you still at the hospital?"

"No. There was nothing we could do, so I brought him back to the house. He and Poppy are out on the terrace right now." She gave a wry laugh. "He's processing everything. At least this will give him something other than the lost baby to talk about."

"Are you okay to stay there with him?"

It was a few seconds before Ginny replied. "I'm fine with this for the short-term, a day or two. We've all known this day would come, but we've never decided how we'll manage if something happens to Mom. I guess it's time to make those decisions."

She was right. How were they going to handle this? Neither of them could take six weeks off from the winery, and Lexi was just as busy.

"Have you called Lexi about this?" he asked.

"No. You know I always go to you first."

Under normal circumstances he thrived on being everyone's go-to person. Right now he didn't feel like the person to be doling out advice. "Should we drive up this afternoon?"

"There's nothing you can do for Mom right now, but I'm sure she'd like to see both of you tomorrow. I'll call you when she's out of surgery and let you know how she's doing."

"Thanks. I have some…ah…business to take care of this afternoon. Lexi's in on it, too, so I can let her know about Mom. Then we should drive up tonight."

"That would be great. I'm sure Ben would be reassured to have everyone here, and I'd really appreciate it, too."

"No problem." He remembered something else she'd said at the beginning of the call. "You said you had some good news, too."

"That's right. I did." Her voice sounded unexpectedly upbeat.

"And…?"

"And…I just found out I'm pregnant again."

"Oh, Ginny. That's wonderful. How are you feeling?"

"I saw the doctor first thing this morning and he confirmed it. He wants me to take things easy, especially for the first trimester, but otherwise I'm fine."

"Looking after Mom and Ben isn't taking it easy, Ginny. Lexi and I will be there as soon as we can. We'll stay with Ben tonight so you can go home and follow doctor's orders."

"Now you sound like Paul."

"Paul's a good guy."

"He is, and so are you. How's Jess?"

Under different circumstances he might have confided in her, but she had enough to cope with, and he wasn't in the mood for another sisterly lecture. If she knew what he'd done, she would try to clean up his mess, too.

"She's fine," he lied. "I'll probably talk to her later this afternoon."

"Tell her I said hi."

"Will do. I'd better give Lexi a call. Let me know if you need anything, okay?"

"Okay. See you tonight, Michael."

After he ended the call, he checked messages to see if Jess had left one. She hadn't, of course. For once he had to wait for someone else to clean up the mess he'd made, and he didn't like it.

JESS WAS A WRECK by the time she got back to the bar. On the ride from Nob Hill, her thoughts had raced through a confused maze of anxiety about losing her grandfather's business, having inherited her mother's inability to judge a man's character, and total disbelief that Michael had turned out to be so manipulative and deceitful. That was the part that hurt the most, because he'd seemed so sincere.

Except for Eric, the place was empty, and for once she was grateful. His look of mild confusion at her early return quickly changed to concern when he saw her. "Jess? What's wrong?"

She wanted to say something, but she couldn't speak. She shook her head instead, and then she burst into tears. Eric rushed over and put his arms around her. "Must be something big," he said, holding her while she sobbed. "In all the years I've known you, I've only seen you cry once."

That had been at her grandfather's funeral. Saying goodbye to him had broken her heart, but this was a million times worse. Michael hadn't just broken her heart. He had ripped it out and smashed it into a bazillion little pieces. And he'd done it on purpose.

After she sucked it up and got herself somewhat under control, Eric sat her in a chair. "I'll be right back," he said, looking mildly disgusted when she wiped her eyes and nose on the sleeve of her jacket. He locked the door and flipped on the closed sign, then he went behind the bar. He came back with a couple of ounces of Scotch in a glass and a handful of napkins. He pulled a chair around to face her and put the glass in her hand. "Drink some of this."

She took a generous gulp and sputtered a little as it heated her throat on its way down. Eric pressed some napkins into her hand so she could mop up the tears and blow her nose. She took another swig of Scotch, and felt herself slowly regaining some self-control.

He gave her the time she needed.

"It's Michael," she said.

Eric's concern shifted to alarm. "Did something happen to him?"

"Not yet," she said. "But it will."

"I don't understand."

"He screwed me over." She blew her nose again. "I was waiting for him…and then Lexi showed up…she's the mystery woman who was here a couple of weeks ago…and…" She started to sob again, but still managed to tell Eric the whole crappy story.

Eric took her glass and set it on the table, then took both her hands in his. "I'm so sorry, hon, but…are you sure? Don't you think you should talk to—"

"I am *not* talking to him *ever* again. When I met him, he asked if I would consider selling the place to him and my answer was no. So what did he do? He sent his sister here to snoop around. Then they sabotaged my chance of getting a building permit. Ugh!" She smacked her forehead. "I should have figured this out from the get-go instead of falling for his stupid pickup lines."

Eric wasn't convinced. "I still think you should talk to him, get his side of the story. I've seen how he looks at you, hon. The guy's crazy about you."

Jess swallowed the last mouthful of Scotch and set the glass on the table next to the pile of soggy napkins. "No, he isn't. That was all part of the plan to trick me into letting him have what he wants. He's *not* getting it."

Thank God she hadn't slept with him. Except, damn it, even after what he'd done, that was something she would always regret.

Chapter Twelve

Jess changed into her work clothes and squirreled herself away in the bar's dimly lit, cluttered little office, ostensibly working on the accounts but without actually accomplishing a damn thing. Eric, trying to make light of the whole horrible mess, had asked how long she planned to sulk. She wasn't sulking, at least not yet. That would come, but it was still too soon. She was too mad, and too frequently on the verge of tears to feel sorry for herself. In the two hours since she'd stormed out of Michael's restaurant, she had oscillated between blind anger and devastating disappointment.

How could Michael do something like this? All the things he'd said to her in the past few weeks kept running through her head, as if they were on automatic replay. Had there been any truth in any of it?

I had a hunch that discussing this project with you over dinner would pay off.

You're amazing.

I'm a patient man and I'll wait till you're ready.

The first time I make love to a woman, I like it to be in a bed.

All lies. Why did she let herself fall for that crap? Because she was an idiot, just like her mother. She'd let herself get caught up in the dream that a man like Michael—an attractive, wealthy family man—was genuinely interested in her, and she had overlooked what he was really after.

She thumbed through a stack of bills—bills she could have paid if she'd been able to get the building permit and qualify for a loan—and set them back on the desk.

Face it, Jess. You've been living a lie. Even worse, she'd duped herself into believing she could make ends meet, that if she could just attract a few more customers, she could get caught up on the bills and fix up the place and, for the first time, her life would be perfect. She'd have a successful business and a man who loved and respected her. Now it was painfully obvious that if business didn't pick up, there was no way she could make ends meet, let alone fix the plumbing. And if she didn't get the restrooms working again, the city might shut her down.

She stared at the computer monitor. She was *not* going to cry. There was no way would she give in to tears again. But the stupid columns of numbers blurred anyway. She wiped her eyes on the sleeve of her sweatshirt and covered her face with her hands. "I'm so sorry, Granddad. I never meant to disappoint you."

She thought about calling Rory or Paige, but they were both at work. Besides, she wasn't ready to share this. They would insist on coming over and she was way too angry to be with anyone right now.

Eric poked his head into the office. "How are you doing?"

"Fine."

"Liar."

She ignored that. "Is it getting busy out there?" The front door had opened and closed a few times and she'd heard Eric chatting with customers.

"I can handle it. And I know you're busy cooking the books, but there's someone here to see you."

To her annoyance, she felt her heart speed up. "I don't want to see him. Tell him to take a hike."

"It's not Michael. In fact, it's not a *him* at all. Come and see for yourself."

"Did you call one of my friends?"

Eric rolled his eyes. "Give me a little credit."

"Who is it?"

He shrugged. "I've never seen her before. Now, get that adorable little tush of yours out there. Besides, I could use a break."

"Okay, I'll be right there." She straightened the paperwork she'd been attempting to work on and turned off the computer monitor. On her way out of the office, she glanced in the mirror. Her eyes were still a little puffy, but most of the redness was gone. She couldn't imagine who wanted to see her, unless it was another health inspector, ready to slap a condemned sign on the door.

She was completely unprepared to see Lexi Morgan sitting at the bar, drinking coffee. She had a lot of nerve, showing up here.

"Hi, Jess. How are you?"

"Did Michael send you?"

She looked down at her cup. "No, I offered."

Jess spun around and would have headed back to the office if Eric hadn't grabbed her shoulders. "I think you should hear her out." He gently steered her behind the bar, poured her a cup of coffee and set it on the counter opposite Lexi's. "Be nice," he whispered. "And behave." Then he disappeared into the kitchen.

Lexi got right to the point. "Michael called me a while ago and told me that you were at the Nob Hill wine bar when I was there, and then you bolted. Figuring out you'd overheard my telephone conversation wasn't much of a leap."

"You came here to admit you bribed someone at city hall to—"

"Hey, I did *not* bribe anyone. I just…put up a few roadblocks."

"Oh, well, that makes it all right."

"I'm not proud of myself, but I was trying to help my brother, and he was trying to help you."

That was the lamest excuse ever. "How was that supposed to help me?"

"You told Michael you were having financial problems. Selling to him would have solved that."

Jess picked up her coffee cup and sloshed some of it on the counter, her hands were shaking so badly. She set the cup down and wiped up the spill. "That's an insult." She tossed the cloth into the bar sink and turned to leave.

Lexi reached across the counter and put a hand on her arm. "I know you're disappointed—"

Jess swung back to face him, angrier than ever. "Disappointed doesn't even come close. I knew he wanted to buy the Whiskey Sour. I told him it wasn't for sale and I thought he understood that, then this afternoon I find out that he's still trying to swindle me out of this place."

Lexi withdrew her hand. "He bought the other building, you know. He put an offer on it this morning and it was accepted. The deal's being finalized this afternoon. He was going to tell you about it at lunch today, and then he was going to make you a different offer. When we met this afternoon, he was going to tell me to back off. If he'd told me sooner, that phone call you overhead never would have happened."

They had been plotting against her, and that was unforgivable. Even so, she had to ask, "What was he going to offer me?"

"You said something at Thanksgiving that changed his mind. So he bought the building on Folsom Street, and he was going to ask me to fast-track your building permit—as you know, I have connections." She even looked a little sheepish as she said it. "And then he wanted me to work with you on the redesign."

"Oh." That was a surprise, but why should she believe it?

"Let me explain a few things about my brother. He's been working in the family business since he was a kid, and he loves it. He did a business degree when he went to college and he was all for expanding the company then, but our father wanted it to stay the small family business it had always been. After he died, Michael took over and I have to tell you, that man has the Midas touch. He's ambitious, sometimes aggressively so, but he's also honest, Jess. He didn't set out to do anything underhanded, and he would never do anything against the law. His biggest mistake was asking me to help. I took that and ran with it."

Jess wasn't buying it. "That makes him just as guilty."

"No, it doesn't. That's not how Michael does business. If he was really determined to buy this place, he would have made an offer you couldn't refuse. Instead…and I don't know if I should tell you this, but what the hell. He was at the bank this morning, arranging financing for the new building, and he looked into backing a loan for you, too."

Jess was stunned. "Um…why would he do that?"

Lexi shrugged. "You'll have to ask him. He can be generous to a fault, but he's never done anything like this before."

Jess relaxed a little and picked up her coffee again. This time it stayed in the cup. "He shouldn't be doing any of this behind my back."

"I agree. It was an arrogant, macho guy thing to do and he realizes how dumb it was. While we're talking about this, I'll let you in on a little secret. Michael has a terrible track record with women."

That was hard to believe.

Lexi leaned toward her and wrapped both hands around her coffee cup. "He'll kill me if he finds out I told you this, but he was pretty serious about someone right after college and she really took him for a ride. Ever since then he's been wary about women who are only interested in his money, and you'd be surprised how many there are."

"I'm not one of them!" She didn't know why she was suddenly on the defensive, either, because *she* hadn't done anything wrong.

"No one thinks you are. Not me, and certainly not Michael." She leaned even closer. "I hope you'll give him a chance to explain…and to apologize…because he realizes he screwed up."

Jess didn't know what to say. Was Lexi telling her the truth? Would Michael? She'd been falling fast and hard for Michael Morgan, and if there was a possibility that he felt the same way, maybe she owed it to both of them to give him another chance.

"Will you talk to him?" Lexi asked. "At least let him explain."

"Fine. I'll talk to him, but he has to come here…this afternoon…while Eric is still here." She hiked a thumb in the direction of the kitchen. No way would she agree to be alone with Michael. He was too charming and too damn sexy for his own good, and he had a way of distracting her.…

"I'll let him know." Lexi glanced at her wristwatch. "I'd better get going. I still have a lot of work to do this afternoon, and Ginny called to tell us my mom is having an emergency appendectomy, so Michael and I are heading up there this evening to stay with our brother."

Jess's anger melted away. "I'm so sorry. Will she be okay? How's Ben handling it?"

"He's a bit upset. My sister is staying with him right now, but she just found out this morning that she's pregnant again."

"Wow, that's exciting." Jess was genuinely happy for her. Ginny would be a wonderful mother, and she certainly had a good role model.

"I'm so thrilled for her. She and Paul really want to start a family, but she's had two miscarriages, so her doctor is strongly advising her to take things easy, avoid stress and get plenty of rest." Lexi took her wallet out of her bag.

"Please, don't worry about it," Jess said, shaking her head emphatically. "I'm so sorry to hear about your mom."

"Thanks." She put her wallet away and slid off the

bar stool. "I'm sure she'll be fine, but she'll need some recovery time. The problem will be finding someone who can help with Ben."

Lexi shrugged. "It's our fault. We've kept him pretty sheltered, though, and that was a mistake."

Jess came out from behind the bar and walked to the door with Lexi. "Poor Ben. I wish there was something I could do."

"For now, letting Michael set things straight will help." Lexi offered her hand and Jess accepted the handshake. "You're okay with me calling him and telling him to come and talk to you?"

Jess nodded. "Thanks for coming," she said a little reluctantly.

"Thanks for seeing me." She glanced around the bar. "If you decide to…well, I'll just say this would be a fun project."

Eric reappeared after she left, and Jess could tell he'd listened in on most of their conversation. "Don't start with me," she warned.

"Wouldn't dream of it."

She headed for the office. "If anyone else shows up, I'll be in here."

Eric grinned. "You got it. Unless maybe you'd like to go home and change your clothes, fix your hair…"

She stopped in the doorway and swung around. "What part of 'don't start with me' didn't you understand?"

He laughed. "What was I thinking? You look…unbelievable."

"Michael is coming here to apologize. He's the one who needs to make a good impression."

"And I'm sure he will. Now go and finish sulking and I'll fix you something to eat."

Chapter Thirteen

Michael parked behind Jess's red Vespa. Instead of getting out, he sat for a minute and rehearsed his apology one last time. After Lexi had called to say Jess had agreed to see him, he hadn't wasted any time getting here. The most he could hope for now was that she wasn't having second thoughts, and that he would sound as sincere as he felt.

If Jess had been any other woman, his apology would have been accompanied by an expensive piece of jewelry, or at least an enormous bouquet of flowers. Jess was no ordinary woman, though, and he already knew better than to show up bearing gifts. They would not be well received. Lexi had also warned him about using excuses, but when it came down to it, there was no excusing his behavior. With any luck, she would accept his apology, and then maybe she would consider his new proposition.

One step at a time, he reminded himself.

Eric was behind the bar, and Larry and Bill were in their usual seats. There was no sign of Jess. The two mechanics greeted him cautiously. Apparently, they'd been told how badly he screwed up. Eric was smiling, though, and Michael took that to be a good sign.

"She's in the office," he said, pointing to the door that was slightly ajar. "Can I get you something? A beer, maybe?"

Michael just wanted to get this over with. "No, thanks." Maybe later, if he was lucky.

He tapped lightly on the door.

"What."

He went in and closed it.

She was sitting on an old oak banker's chair with her back to the door. She didn't turn around.

"Jess?"

The chair creaked and then groaned as she slowly swiveled to face him. Her eyes were red rimmed and a little puffy as though she'd been crying, and her lips were locked into a thin line. On the way over here, he had figured out exactly what he needed to say to her, all the while thinking he couldn't possibly feel like more of an idiot. Wrong. Seeing her like this made him feel like the insensitive, arrogant ass he clearly was.

"I'm so sorry." Damn. That was *not* what he'd planned to say. *I'm sorry* never sounded sincere.

"You should be."

He didn't want to smile, but he couldn't help himself.

"This is not funny."

"You're right. It isn't. I've made a complete mess of things, Jess, and I really am sorry." Ugh, he'd said it again.

Her mouth softened a little. "You had no business interfering in *my* business, and one more thing. If I need help, I'll ask for it."

He wondered what it would take to make her smile. "When was the last time you asked anyone for help?"

She had to think about that. "Once in a while my friends Rory and Paige help me figure out what to wear."

He had not expected her to say that, and it made him laugh. He couldn't help it. In an old green-and-navy-plaid shirt over a gray T-shirt, she looked like a cross between a teenage tomboy and a construction worker. Her high-tops were untied and one of the knees of her jeans had the makings of a hole in it. "If I had to guess, I'd say today wasn't one of those days."

"You're kind of on thin ice here." Laugh lines appeared around her eyes, though. "I'm not a fashion plate and I never pretended to be."

Would she believe him if he told her that he liked what he saw? Not likely. "Getting back to my apology…I want you to know it was never my intention to hurt you. I convinced myself that getting you to sell this place was in your best interest. It was stupid and arrogant and I'm…" He couldn't keep saying he was sorry. "I was wrong."

He wanted to tell her that he'd like to help her get back on her feet, but it was too soon for that. Hell, he had to face facts—he might never get the chance. But he could make an offer, at least in a general way. "If there's anything I can do to help…to undo the trouble I've caused you…I hope you'll let me."

"Lexi said you had something in mind."

She sounded interested, and he figured it was now or never. "Building permits, bank loans, I can help with all of that, if you'll let me."

He watched the emotions flicker across her face. Uncertainty, consideration and finally a decision. Even before she spoke, he knew her answer wouldn't be what he wanted to hear.

"It's tempting, but I can't accept."

He was a man who didn't like to take no for an answer, so he really had to struggle against his natural instinct to make her change her mind.

"You understand why, right?"

He didn't, and he might as well tell her. What did he have to lose? "There are no strings, Jess."

"But the thing is, you hardly know me. And it's not like we're…" She stopped and looked away.

"We're not what?"

She shrugged and her face went pink.

Sleeping together? Is that what she was going to say? He couldn't decide if he should be flattered or offended. He wanted her in his life and yes, he'd certainly like to have her in his bed, but that's not what this was about. "I know you well enough to say I'd like to know you better. And what you said about why your family business is so important…that's what motivates me."

She looked less guarded, as though she might even forgive him, and then the uncertainty in her eyes was replaced with guilt and she shook her head. "I can't. It feels too risky, especially for you."

He knew she didn't see herself as being a good businesswoman, but he'd seen her in the bar with her customers and she was in her element. And she didn't have to agree to his offer right now, he reminded himself. The important thing now was to regain her trust.

He took a step into the small, cluttered space. He wanted to touch her, and if she'd let him get close, he might get her to open up again. And then his phone rang. He would have turned it off or left it in the car if he hadn't been waiting for a call from Ginny. And this call was from her.

"I'm sorry," he said. "It's my family. I really have to take it."

She shrugged.

"Ginny, hi," he said without taking his eyes off Jess. "How's Mom?"

"The hospital just called. She's out of surgery and everything went well. They said she's awake but still groggy."

"Are you still at the house?"

"I am. Mom's in good hands and I don't want to take Ben back to the hospital."

"Is he there with you now?"

"No, he's outside with the dog. I asked him to take her out because I don't want him to hear me talking about Mom and the hospital."

Jess was listening intently, and in such a small space, there was a good chance she could hear both sides of the conversation.

"Good idea."

"Do you know when you'll be home?"

"Ah...I'm in a meeting right now. I'll leave in an hour or so."

"Wonderful. I told Ben you were coming."

"I'm guessing he wants to work on the car." He caught Jess's smile.

"No, but you might be surprised by what he did say."

"What's that?"

"He said, 'Mikey's bringing Jessie.'"

That made him laugh, and he could tell from Jess's widening grin that she'd heard it, too.

Their gazes locked.

"Can't hurt to ask," he said.

Her eyebrows shot up.

"Are you serious?" Ginny asked.

"Of course I'm serious. I'll let you know what she says."

Jess lowered her eyebrows and knitted them together.

He took advantage of her unabashed eavesdropping and silent questions to take a step closer. He ended the call and took another step, stopping in front of her so she had to tip her head back to look up at him. He put his phone in his pocket and held out one hand.

Would she take it?

She did.

Her skin felt soft and cool. He helped her up and held his ground, and when she was standing there was only a narrow space between them. The chair and desk behind her prevented her from backing away, but she didn't seem to mind. "That was Ginny. My mother had to have an emergency appendectomy today. She's in the hospital."

"Lexi told me. I'm glad to hear she's okay."

"What else did you hear?"

"That Ben asked for me. That's so sweet."

He took her other hand. "Ben has good taste in women."

Finally she smiled for real. He squeezed her hands and resisted the temptation to kiss her. She was coming around, but she wasn't there yet.

"I wish you were coming home with me," he said.

"Are you serious?"

"Of course I am. We…my sisters and I…we've been

afraid something like this was going to happen. Ben's a great kid, but he's been very sheltered and he has a really tough time coping with any disruption to his routine. Ginny's staying with him right now, but we have to find someone to come and help with Ben while our mother recuperates."

"Are you asking me to go with you?"

"What would your answer be if I did?"

"If you want to find out, I guess you'll have to ask."

After everything that had happened today, he couldn't believe she wanted him to. He turned her hands over in his and slowly drew the pads of his thumbs across her palms. "Will you come home with me tonight?"

Without hesitation, she nodded. "I will if Eric will cover for me."

Kissing her no longer seemed risky—it seemed like the right to do—so he lowered his head and touched her lips with his. He kept it light and quick, which wasn't easy when she kissed him back.

"Does this mean you're done being mad at me?" he asked.

"I'm getting there."

"That makes me a lucky man," he said.

"But if you *ever* do anything like this again…"

Not in a million years. "I've learned my lesson."

"I can take care of myself."

"I get that." He admired her determination and independence, but he would also love to give her the things she'd had to live without.

"Good."

"So…you'll talk to Eric about tonight?"

"I'm sure he won't mind. I'll ask him right now."

Michael hoped Eric would agree, because he was already formulating a new plan, one that involved Jess and his family, and a lot more than just one night.

Idiot, he chided himself. *Here you go again. Hatching a plan that involves her, but without discussing it with her.* He'd learned a couple of valuable lessons today. He couldn't make decisions for her, and he needed to slow down and take things one day at a time. His father used to say, *Good things come to those who wait.* He finally understood, and he really hoped his father was right.

Chapter Fourteen

For the past five weeks, Jess had felt as though she'd been living someone else's life, and tonight was no exception.

Morgan's at the Wharf was decked out for New Year's Eve, and from the floor-to-ceiling windows that overlooked the bay and the Golden Gate Bridge, Jess waited for the countdown and fireworks to begin. Michael stood behind her, both arms wrapped snugly around her waist. She leaned back against him, her head resting comfortably on his shoulder. Of everything that had happened, there was no question that being with him was the hardest to believe.

Although the part about "being with him" was being used in the loosest possible sense of the term. All these weeks she had been living in his mother's house and sleeping in his mother's guest room, and *nothing* had happened. Without actually saying it again, his rule about what *wasn't* going to happen in a bed in his mother's house was apparently carved in stone. In spite of several hot and heavy make-out sessions, they still hadn't made love, but that was about to change…tonight. She'd shaved her legs and everything.

She'd gone up to the valley when Sophia was in the

hospital because Ben had asked for her. And, yes, because in spite of what Michael and Lexi had done, she still wanted to be with him. Once she was there, he'd made her an offer she couldn't refuse.

She would stay with Ben and his mother, and while she was there, she would close the bar and Lexi would oversee the renovations. Michael and Lexi, true to their word, were the well-connected masters of fast-tracking. Jess was blown away by what they had accomplished in such a short time. Every day Lexi was in touch by phone, getting her approval on things and sending photographs by email so she could keep up with all the changes at the Whiskey Sour. Once a week Ginny spent the day with her mother and brother so Jess could run down to the city and see the progress firsthand. Just this week the turquoise booths had been installed, and they were even more perfect than Jess had imagined.

Tonight, Ginny and her husband had offered to stay at the house with Sophia and Ben so Jess could come to the New Year's Eve party at the wine bar on the wharf. The week before Christmas she had come into the city for a day of shopping with Rory and she'd found the dress she was wearing tonight—a sleek, long-sleeved, scoop-necked dream of a dress in a deep shade of teal-blue with just a hint of sparkle. It was the first truly dressy dress she'd ever bought for herself, and she loved it. Rory's one concession had been with the shoes. Jess had insisted on flats because she was more comfortable in them, and because she secretly liked giving Michael the advantage of being that much taller.

She had finally met a man who looked at her in a way that made her bones melt. From the beginning he'd been clear about what he wanted, and yet he had shown remarkable restraint. He made her *want* to be touched, and that was a new experience for her. So far he hadn't said anything about her dress, though. His eyes and his hands had done all the talking.

Tonight they were staying in the city. They hadn't exactly talked about it, but her suitcase was already in his apartment, and when they got there, the rule about not making love in a bed in his mother's house did not apply. And if he had any doubts about whether or not it was going to happen, she just happened to be wearing a seductively sexy pale pink bra and matching panties that would seal the deal. Rory had said they were meant to be put on so they could be taken off, and she must be right because they were the least comfortable things Jess had ever worn. More than once that evening she had contemplated taking them off and going commando, except she wasn't a commando kind of girl.

A waiter appeared at their side with a tray of champagne flutes. Without letting her go, Michael took two glasses from the tray and set them on the table next to them. "Thanks, Dylan," he said to the young man. "Happy New Year." And then he slid his arm around her again.

Jess rotated her head slightly so she could look up at him. "Do you know the names of *all* your employees?"

"It's one of the lessons my father and grandfather taught me. If you're not on a first-name basis with all of your employees, then your company is too big to qualify as a family business."

He never ceased to amaze her. "Sounds like something my granddad would have said, but he only had a handful of people working for him. Will the fireworks start exactly at midnight?"

"On the stroke of twelve."

It would be the perfect end to a perfect year in—she craned her neck to see the big clock behind the orchestra—four minutes. She caught a glimpse of Rory and Mitch on the dance floor, then Nicola and Jonathan swung into view. "Thank you for inviting my friends to join us tonight. It's been great having them here."

"They seem to be enjoying themselves."

"What's not to enjoy? Everything—the food, wine, music, decorations—it's all perfect." She'd been thrilled that they had all decided to ring in the New Year together. She scanned the crowd, looking for Paige and Andy. She didn't know where they'd disappeared to, but she was sure they'd reappear to see the fireworks. Maria and Tony were sitting together on a banquette near the windows, Maria snug and secure in the protective circle of her husband's arm. Lexi was there, too, and since she claimed to be between boyfriends, she'd talked Eric into coming with her. The two of them had struck up a friendship while working together on the renovations at the Whiskey Sour.

In lots of ways, Jess still felt like the awkward girl in the strapless gown who'd caught Michael's eye at Rory and Mitch's wedding. In so many others, she felt as though she'd been transformed into a woman with a promising business, a family and a man who appeared to be as much in love with her as she was with him.

The clock showed one minute to midnight.

Michael moved beside her. She felt chilled now that his body heat wasn't mingling with hers.

"There's something I need to ask you," he said.

The band riffed a familiar tune that segued into the countdown. "Ten!...nine!..."

She smiled up at him. "Ask away."

"Eight!...seven!...six!..."

He slipped an arm around her waist. "I love you, Jess." It was exactly what she'd dreamed he would say someday and the one thing she hadn't dared to hope for.

"Five!...four!...three!...two!..."

"Will you marry me?"

"One!"

"Yes. Yes!" She was vaguely aware of an explosion of lights over the bay and the cheers of "Happy New Year" around them, but they could have been miles away. The only tangible thing was the warmth of Michael's lips on hers.

She tipped her head back and looked at him. "Are you serious?" And had she really said yes?

"I wouldn't joke around about something like this."

Neither would she, and she had just said yes. Talk about getting caught up in the moment. "But...we haven't known each other very long."

"You should know me well enough by now to have figured out that when I want something, I go for it."

True. He was nothing if not confident.

"You could also think of this as part of our bargain. I still owe you." He pulled a jeweler's box from his pocket.

"What bargain?"

"The one where you agreed to look after my family. I figure the least I can do is offer to make you part of it."

"I thought that's what the Whiskey Sour was for." It

was the most lavish, over-the-top thank-you gift she'd ever received.

"That's just an investment." He opened the box and she felt her eyes go wide. "I hope you like it. Rory and Paige helped me pick it out."

The elegant simplicity of the ring was a perfect choice, although she'd never actually seen a diamond that big outside a jewelry-store window. Michael slipped it onto her left hand.

"I love it." She couldn't take her eyes off it. "But are you sure? I mean…" A warm flush raced up her throat and across her face. "We still haven't…"

He lowered his head and laughed softly into her ear. "I don't need to sleep with you to know I want to spend the rest of my life with you." His breath did shivery things to her ear. "Besides, I promised to wait until you're ready, remember?"

She was *so* ready…and she had the underwear to prove it. She wrapped her arms around his neck. "I was thinking tonight…"

"Tonight it is." He kissed her, and everyone cheered and applauded. Then he let her go, handed a champagne flute to her and raised his in the air.

A small crowd had gathered around them—his sister and Eric and her friends. "She said yes!" Michael announced.

Everyone cheered and raised their glasses. They had all been in on this? Her friends hugged her and gushed over her ring, and Jess floated through the rest of the evening as if she was on a cloud.

Michael slipped an arm around her shoulder. "Thank you."

"For what?"

"For saying yes."

She realized there was one thing she hadn't said. "I love you."

He put his arms around her and kissed her. "Are you ready to go home?"

"I'm ready." And she was.

Epilogue

Six months later…

"After all your grumbling about wearing a strapless dress at my wedding and at Rory's, I can't believe you chose one for yourself," Nicola said.

Jess gave the skirt a little swoosh. "This is the new me."

"Hold still." Maria fussed with the graceful sweep of the train.

"A new and absolutely gorgeous you," Rory said. "I can't believe it was the first dress you tried on."

When Rory got married last fall, she had tried on every dress in San Francisco. Not because she was having trouble finding *the* dress, but because she loved trying on dresses.

"It was the *only* dress I tried on. Sometimes a girl just gets lucky." She had set out to find the impossible. Something classy and modest and sexy. Something that matched her newfound appreciation for being a woman. Something that worked with her slender, subtle curves and didn't require cleavage, since she didn't have any. She'd known this was the dress the moment she walked into the shop, and she'd fallen in love with it before it was even off the hanger.

"What's luck got to do with it?" Rory asked. "If it wasn't for me, this wedding wouldn't be happening."

"How do you figure that?" Jess asked.

"You met Michael at my wedding, remember? And it was all thanks to that beautiful strapless dress you were wearing."

Jess laughed. "No offense, Rory, but I think it was *in spite of* the dress, not because of it."

A waiter appeared at the door with a tray of five champagne flutes. "Thank you, Simon." She passed the glasses to her four bridesmaids and took the last one for herself. "You've all been wonderful and I wanted to give you all a thank-you toast before the ceremony."

"This was *so* meant to be," Paige said. "You and Michael are like our very own version of *My Fair Lady*."

"That would make me Eliza Doolittle."

"Or Audrey Hepburn," Rory said. "You've got to love that."

Maria handed Jess a bouquet of pink roses and gave an exaggerated sigh. "And you have to admit that Michael makes an especially dreamy Professor Higgins."

True. Every day he told her she was the most beautiful woman in the world. It didn't matter that it wasn't true, because he believed it was, and he made her believe it, too. He was an exceptional tutor in every way imaginable and in some ways she never would have imagined. It had taken some time to accept that such an amazing man had invited her to share his life, and she was quite certain she would always feel a little like Cinderella—no, make that Eliza Doolittle—a little afraid that someone would pinch her and she'd wake up behind the bar at the

Whiskey Sour, wearing a pair of old jeans and a man's flannel shirt.

Last winter her granddad's legacy had undergone an amazing transition, thanks to Lexi's incredible design talent. She had taken Jess's dream of a fifties-themed cocktail lounge and turned it into a turquoise-and-cream reality. Jess loved it and she knew her grandfather would have, too.

"To us," she said. "Thanks for always being here for me."

"To us."

"To you and Michael."

"To love and marriage."

"To happily ever after."

The clink of crystal and sips of champagne were followed by a group hug.

"Michael is also one very lucky man," Maria said. "You should see what she's wearing underneath this dress. These two are going to have quite a honeymoon."

"I was with her when she bought that lingerie," Rory said. "It's going to knock Michael's socks off."

"You guys are hopeless." But they were right. Who knew that dressing to please a man could give her so much…pleasure?

Paige gave her a hug. "Sorry, sweetie. We're all just a little jealous. Have you figured out where he's taking you on your honeymoon?"

"No, and it's killing me, but he really wanted this to be a surprise, so I told him to go for it."

"That would make me crazy," Nic said. "How did you know what to pack?"

"Lexi packed for me. And you know…I'm not

complaining. It's been a busy couple of months and that was one less thing I had to do."

"Is Eric managing the bar while you're away?" Paige asked.

"Yes, and Ben is staying with Ginny and Paul. Ginny's baby isn't due for another six weeks, so that's worked out perfectly. Then he'll come and live with Michael and me in the city. We found a great program for him and he loves being part of it." Ben's increasing independence had been a slow and not always smooth transition, but in the end it had worked out.

"How is Michael's mother handling the changes?"

"She's getting used to the idea of being on her own, and she's looking forward to being a grandmother."

"You're amazing," Maria said. "Ben's a lucky kid."

"I'm the lucky one." Ben's self-confidence had blossomed in the past few months. He was excited at the prospect of being Michael's best man, and he'd been thrilled to have them use "his car" for the wedding.

Maria pointed to the clock on the dresser. "We need to get downstairs. It's time to get started."

Jess followed her four best friends down the stairs of Michael's family home and waited with them near the French doors. The music swelled and one by one her friends entered the courtyard, and then it was her turn. She stepped outside into the sunshine, vaguely aware of the people seated on white folding chairs but with eyes for only one man. Michael's smile widened when he saw her, and as his gaze traveled over her, his eyes let her know exactly what he was thinking.

Strapless gowns totally rule.

* * * * *

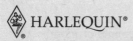 HARLEQUIN®

 *American ★ Romance*®

COMING NEXT MONTH

Available February 8, 2011

#1341 ROUGHNECK COWBOY
American Romance's Men of the West
Marin Thomas

#1342 THE RANCHER'S TWIN TROUBLES
The Buckhorn Ranch
Laura Marie Altom

#1343 HIS VALENTINE SURPRISE
Fatherhood
Tanya Michaels

#1344 OFFICER DADDY
Safe Harbor Medical
Jacqueline Diamond

REQUEST YOUR FREE BOOKS!

2 FREE NOVELS PLUS 2 FREE GIFTS!

HARLEQUIN®

American ★ Romance®

Love, Home & Happiness!

YES! Please send me 2 FREE Harlequin® American Romance® novels and my 2 FREE gifts (gifts are worth about $10). After receiving them, if I don't wish to receive any more books, I can return the shipping statement marked "cancel." If I don't cancel, I will receive 4 brand-new novels every month and be billed just $4.24 per book in the U.S. or $4.99 per book in Canada. That's a saving of at least 15% off the cover price! It's quite a bargain! Shipping and handling is just 50¢ per book.* I understand that accepting the 2 free books and gifts places me under no obligation to buy anything. I can always return a shipment and cancel at any time. Even if I never buy another book from Harlequin, the two free books and gifts are mine to keep forever.

154/354 HDN E5LG

Name	(PLEASE PRINT)	
Address		Apt. #
City	State/Prov.	Zip/Postal Code

Signature (if under 18, a parent or guardian must sign)

Mail to the **Harlequin Reader Service:**
IN U.S.A.: P.O. Box 1867, Buffalo, NY 14240-1867
IN CANADA: P.O. Box 609, Fort Erie, Ontario L2A 5X3

Not valid for current subscribers to Harlequin® American Romance® books.

Want to try two free books from another line?
Call 1-800-873-8635 or visit www.morefreebooks.com.

* Terms and prices subject to change without notice. Prices do not include applicable taxes. N.Y. residents add applicable sales tax. Canadian residents will be charged applicable provincial taxes and GST. Offer not valid in Quebec. This offer is limited to one order per household. All orders subject to approval. Credit or debit balances in a customer's account(s) may be offset by any other outstanding balance owed by or to the customer. Please allow 4 to 6 weeks for delivery. Offer available while quantities last.

Your Privacy: Harlequin is committed to protecting your privacy. Our Privacy Policy is available online at www.eHarlequin.com or upon request from the Reader Service. From time to time we make our lists of customers available to reputable third parties who may have a product or service of interest to you. If you would prefer we not share your name and address, please check here. ☐

Help us get it right—We strive for accurate, respectful and relevant communications. To clarify or modify your communication preferences, visit us at www.ReaderService.com/consumerschoice.

HARI0R

Harlequin Romance author Donna Alward is loved for her gorgeous rancher heroes.

Meet Wyatt as he's confronted by both a precious little pink bundle left on his doorstep and his neighbor Elli who's going to show him the ropes....

Introducing
PROUD RANCHER, PRECIOUS BUNDLE

THE SQUAWKING QUIETED as Elli picked the baby up, and Wyatt turned around, trying hard to ignore the feelings of inadequacy as Darcy immediately stopped fussing.

"Maybe she's uncomfortable. What do you think, sweetheart?" Elli turned her conversation to the baby.

"What do you think is wrong?" Wyatt asked, putting the coffee pot back on the burner.

A strange look passed over Elli's face, one that looked like guilt and panic. But it was gone quickly. "I couldn't say," she replied.

"But you were so good with her this afternoon." Wyatt put his hands on his hips.

"Lucky, that's all. I just…remembered a few things." The same strange look flitted over her features once more.

Wyatt took the coffee to the table. "You fooled me. You looked like you knew exactly what you were doing." So much so that Wyatt had felt completely inept. A feeling he despised. He was used to being the one in control.

Elli and Darcy walked the length of the kitchen and back. After a few moments, she admitted, "I haven't really cared for a baby before. The things I thought of were simply things I'd heard about. Not from experience, Mr. Black."

Her chin jutted up, closing the subject but making him

want to ask the questions now pulsing through his mind. But then he remembered the old saying—*Don't look a gift horse in the mouth.* He'd benefit from whatever insight she had and be glad of it.

"I don't really know what babies need," he said. "I fed her, patted her back like you did, walked her to sleep, but every time I put her down…"

Wyatt almost groaned. Of course. He'd forgotten one important thing. He'd been so focused on getting the formula the right temperature that he'd forgotten to check her diaper. Not that he had any clue what to do there either.

Pulling calves and shoveling out stalls was far less intimidating than one tiny newborn.

"She's probably due for a diaper change, isn't she." He tried to sound nonchalant. This was a perfect opportunity. Elli must know how to change a diaper. He could simply watch her so he'd know better for the next time.

Instead, Elli came around the corner of the counter and placed Darcy back in his arms. "Here you go, Uncle Wyatt," she said lightly. "You get diaper duty. I'll fix the coffee. Cream and sugar?"

Oh boy, Wyatt thought, looking down into Darcy's pursed face, his smug plan blown to smithereens. He was in for it now.

Will sparks fly between Elli and Wyatt?

Find out in
PROUD RANCHER, PRECIOUS BUNDLE

Available February 2011 from Harlequin Romance

Try these Healthy and Delicious Spring Rolls!

INGREDIENTS

2 packages rice-paper spring roll wrappers (20 wrappers)

1 cup grated carrot

¼ cup bean sprouts

1 cucumber, julienned

1 red bell pepper, without stem and seeds, julienned

4 green onions finely chopped— use only the green part

DIRECTIONS

1. Soak one rice-paper wrapper in a large bowl of hot water until softened.

2. Place a pinch each of carrots, sprouts, cucumber, bell pepper and green onion on the wrapper toward the bottom third of the rice paper.

3. Fold ends in and roll tightly to enclose filling.

4. Repeat with remaining wrappers. Chill before serving.

Find this and many more delectable recipes including the perfect dipping sauce in